Logan Dory

Dedication

This book stands as a beacon for the millions of hardworking Americans who diligently pay their insurance premiums. Within its pages lies the power to equip you with the knowledge necessary to shield yourself from exploitation and manipulation by insurance carriers.

Table of Contents

About the Author

Throughout my entire journey in the construction industry, starting from the early days, I took on every aspect of the job myself. From plumbing and electrical work to framing, windows, doors, siding, tile, casing, baseboards, molding, flooring, kitchens, bathrooms, dry walling, finishing – you name it. Even tasks like painting, the trade that many carpenters tend to dislike, I tackled head-on. It's only when you invest time in actually performing these tasks that you come to truly appreciate the skills required.

I've framed, wired, & plumb roughed entire homes, making countless mistakes along the way. Yet, each mistake was a lesson learned, leading to multiple attempts until I reached a point of perfection. Fast forward to now, and I find myself dealing with aches and pains in my shoulders, knees, ankles, and hands, battling tendonitis, carpal tunnel, and arthritis – the physical toll of my years of hands-on work. However, the wealth of knowledge I've gained allows me to confidently estimate the time and cost involved in any project.

Being a skilled estimator is not just about crunching numbers; it's about understanding every nuance of the trade. I've transitioned from a hands-on role to a project manager, overseeing thousands of projects. In this journey, I made mistakes, honed my skills, and climbed the ranks to become a senior project manager. The same evolution occurred in my estimation skills. I've mastered every aspect of the industry, particularly within the insurance field.

When I read through documents or someone else's estimate, I can discern immediately whether it's crafted by a seasoned estimator or someone with a surface-level understanding of the industry. The ability to spot well-written estimates from those that lack crucial information is a testament to the depth of knowledge I've acquired over the years – knowledge that proves invaluable in ensuring successful repairs and projects. I have been fortunate to work as a vender for 20 years and 5 years as a non-vender. This experience has enabled me to understand both perspectives of how everything operates. Now, to their disadvantage, I inform you, the homeowner, to provide you with knowledge and empower you with information. I took this action because all parties attempt to take advantage of a claim, and this industry needs correction.

I hope this information will address some of the issues. Ultimately, none of these parties wants you, the homeowner, to have this knowledge. Despite my attempts to communicate with the carriers and provide a solution, it seems to have fallen on deaf ears.

The Harsh Truth...

Navigating the challenging reality of the insurance industry demands careful consideration of various perspectives on handling losses. In this sector, cultivating relationships is pivotal, particularly for Public Adjusters like myself who stand on your side. Our shared objective is securing what you rightfully deserve, although our individual approaches may differ. Over time, reputations play a crucial role, especially when dealing with the same adjuster for subsequent losses. The manner in which you approach the process dictates its speed and resolution—whether efficiently settled or prolonged, potentially leading to appraisal.

Unfortunately, time constraints often hinder a thorough background check of vetting and hiring a Public Adjuster. The decision is often based on verbal communication, assessing conviction, and gauging credibility. Some Public Adjusters adopt an approach of throwing everything at the wall, settling for what sticks, potentially resulting in inflated claims to double the amount paid or more than what is genuinely owed. While this may seem advantageous initially, it can tarnish the adjuster's reputation over time, prompting adjusters to dismiss their estimates and resort to appraisal, further delaying claim settlements.

The temptation to choose a Public Adjuster who operates this way is a choice. However, our extensive experience suggests a more prudent path. Having repeatedly dealt with the same adjusters, they have come to trust the accuracy of our claims, resulting in minimal adjustments or straightforward approvals. We prioritize ethical practices, ensuring that claims accurately reflect losses without exploiting insurance companies or enabling homeowners to profit from their claims. We are putting that experience out here so you can make better-informed decisions.

Ultimately, the decision rests with you. If you seek competence, industry knowledge, and familiarity with insurance company protocols, our proposition is straightforward. Use this information to help you. Our strict adherence to ethical standards, accurate claims, and the freedom to decide on contractors without influence. This information is to give you leverage for that informed decision, potentially saving fees and avoiding undesirable contractual entanglements. This will play into your decision about who you use to repair your home. We explain how we prepare and present your estimate to the claims adjuster, enabling you to choose between the contractor operating out of their home or the large corporation.

It All Comes Down To The Estimate

In the final analysis of your estimates, the pivotal factor boils down to the proficiency of the individual serving as your adjuster and their level of expertise on the carrier side.

For homeowners, it hinges on the capabilities of their contractor or estimator, specifically their proficiency in detailing and crafting a comprehensive repair estimate. Ultimately, the experience and confidence of the individuals on both sides play a decisive role in ensuring you receive the appropriate compensation for your loss.

Regrettably, not every adjuster approaches their role the same way. Some may readily approve an estimate, especially if there is an existing rapport between the contractor/estimator and the adjuster. Conversely, disagreements on the scope of work can arise, leading to a situation where the adjuster obstinately resists despite the estimator's justifications. In such cases, the dispute may escalate to appraisal, wherein the competence of the NEW individual crafting the estimate remains crucial.

Unfortunately, individuals on both sides of this industry often lack extensive experience, leading to the inclusion of unwarranted scope or embellishment of losses. Public Adjusters (PAs) may seek higher payouts by exaggerating the loss, while inexperienced estimators may inflate labor hours to compensate for oversights.

Navigating this landscape requires reaching a justifiable estimate, followed by negotiations between the adjuster and estimator. However, if the estimate is not grounded in justification, the adjuster faces challenges when explaining it to their supervisors. This may trigger the appraisal process again. Due to our long experience when we engage in an appraisal, our estimates typically remain within a 5% margin of the original figure. This is attributed to the meticulous justification of every element within our estimates, backed by extensive experience and knowledge—a level of expertise not universally found in the industry. It's worth noting that while a project manager may provide similar insights, their focus may not necessarily align with estimating or justification of numbers.

Further Explanation

This information offers a concise and accessible understanding of the insurance industry, making it a valuable resource for individuals facing losses at their homes. The promise of quick and practical education without the need for extensive and confusing study is likely to resonate with those seeking clarity in this intricate domain.

Insurance is indeed a complex and extensive field, requiring in-depth knowledge to navigate. Becoming an adjuster, estimator, or contractor involves delving into thousands of pages of information, making it a challenging and convoluted journey. The intricacies of the industry can be overwhelming, and explaining it comprehensively is no small feat.

Fortunately, my 25 years in the insurance industry and 35 years in the construction field have equipped me with a wealth of experience. The information I have gathered condenses what is truly essential for those in the field—

providing insights on what to do, how to handle tasks independently, and effectively managing the people you work with. This knowledge primarily benefits the insured, offering you valuable guidance.

It's worth noting that while the information here may be more beneficial to the insured, some carriers, if not solely focused on profits, could recognize the potential for significant overall loss reduction. Our insights, derived from hands-on experience, provide a straightforward perspective on the insurance claim process when compared to the sometimes lengthy and convoluted resources available.

You Made A Claim!!!

Three outcomes are likely when you file a claim: firstly, your rates may increase; secondly, you could face policy termination; or thirdly, there might be no immediate repercussions. However, in my extensive experience handling thousands of claims, the occurrence of the third option is rare. Even if your rates don't rise immediately, they often do at the time of renewal. Switching to another insurance carrier won't erase the claim from your history; it will remain on your history, leading to higher premiums.

Even if you retract your claim, acknowledging an error and deciding not to proceed, it still becomes part of your claim history. Consequently, seeking coverage with a new carrier will result in higher premiums. If you're ultimately going to bear the cost, ensure you're compensated according to your policy. Whether or not you want to engage in the claims process, you're entitled to receive what your policy dictates. If you fail to assert your rights, the insurance company may avoid making rightful payments. Your insurer's indifference requires you to prioritize your interests, as they won't do you any favors.

Properly Classifying Your Claim

Regardless of the nature of the loss, each peril possesses its own categorizations, dictating distinct approaches to mitigation. Mitigating a fire differs from addressing water damage, and dealing with a puff back involves more than simple wall cleaning. While the term "mold" may instill fear in homeowners, insurance companies view it favorably, as it imposes limits or denials based on policy language. Accurate classification of causes of loss is crucial. Many home backups are misidentified; they are often mainline blockages, a covered peril, while true backups, originating from a septic tank or sewer, have specific limitations. Precision in terminology affects the classification of the loss, making it challenging to alter without justification from a licensed plumber or contractor.

Unintended consequences

Unintended consequences may arise when describing a loss, particularly in the context of insurance policies. It's crucial to carefully examine your policy exclusions, especially concerning the source of the water. Some policies specify that if water damage is caused by an appliance, it may not be covered, or there could be a cap on the coverage, typically around $3000. Filing a claim for such cases might not be advisable, as it could impact your claims history and potentially lead to increased rates. For instance, if the water damage is attributed to sewage water coming up through your toilet, mislabeling it as a ‘backup' can automatically impose a cap on your loss. Understanding the correct terminology is essential for accurately classifying your claim. A 'backup' refers to your septic tank or sewer system pushing sewage into your home due to city issues, rain, or a full septic tank. In contrast, a 'main line blockage' occurs when there's a blockage in the main waste line, causing water to back up into your house, often due to toilet paper stuck in the line.

Exercise caution when using the term 'mold' in the context of water leaks. Mold can grow within 12 to 24 hours, and using the word 'mold' prematurely might lead you to believe there's a mold problem when, in reality, it's a water loss. Mold is often a secondary damage resulting from water leaks, high moisture, or humidity. It's advisable to seek advice from your mitigation company or the vendor recommended by your insurance company before filing a claim to ensure proper classification.

Remember that one word can significantly impact how your claim is processed, potentially putting a cap on it. While the individuals handling your claim are generally just doing their job, understanding and using the correct terminology can prevent unnecessary issues and ensure a smoother claims process.

Before Preceding, It Is Paramount You Read This First

Before you proceed, it is crucial to thoroughly review this section as it holds vital information for homeowners regarding estimating by adjusters, public adjusters, independent adjusters, and the appraisal process. The estimation example presented shortly will tie everything together, emphasizing the significance of understanding the content herein. Be prepared to acknowledge the possibility that your current estimate may lack certain crucial elements, underscoring the importance of having an experienced adjuster to ensure you receive what you are truly owed for your claim. In the absence of an experienced adjustor, I'm offering you the knowledge to handle the adjustor and maximize value yourself.

This information is here to empower your decision-making by providing insights into the pivotal aspects that influence the writing of an estimate. It's essential to grasp that individual adjusters are NOT licensed contractors. Remember, they are often the ones responsible for drafting estimates, especially for losses under $50,000. This applies even when a comparable estimate is written by another contractor or vendor. After reading this section, you will fully understand of the value of investing in this content by taking matters into your own hands and becoming informed. This can help you save money that you would be throwing away to a Public Adjuster.

Example of Tub Tile

Consider the bathroom in your house, with a tub, having an area of approximately 60 to 75 sq ft. The tub area includes various finish components such as wall tile, bullnose tile, soap dishes, a tile towel bar, and thresholds for windows or niches. Now, imagine you have a water loss that damages the bathroom. Outside the tub, there is damage to the drywall & vanity; however, it also affects three of the bullnoses and one wall tile that gets removed during the mitigation. There are three methods for estimating the cost of repairing this tiled area for a home insurance claim. (Yes, there are more items than just the tile, but we are using just the tile in your tub, for example.)

Scenario 1

There's the "remove & replace tile in tub/shower up to 75 square feet" method, presented as a single line item on your estimate with an approximate lump sum price of $2500. This encompasses all components in one comprehensive task.

Scenario 2

Your adjusters may opt for a square-foot pricing method, which involves calculating the total square footage of the tile walls. For example, they might estimate 75 square feet of tile without including any other line items in the estimate. If you just read it as replacing the tile, you would think you are accurately getting paid for the tile in the tub. Yet this approach **excludes** several essential items. If the tub area is to be estimated using this method, then it must account for all elements. It's crucial to add all the individual items like the linear foot of the bullnose, sill measurements, and the inclusion of soap dishes. When you add all of those up, sometimes it's more money than the singular one of just tiling the tub area. One includes everything; the other needs to be broken up. But what insurance adjusters do is they just do the tile by the square foot, and you think you're getting what you're owed. Sometimes, the adjuster may believe they are following the correct procedure. Still, they may not have received proper training in the software they're using, nor do they possess a background in construction to identify all the missing items or understand the true cost of tiling a shower. You would only be getting a fraction of what is owed to replace that tile. When you add in all of the items it now becomes reasonable to pay an installer to complete this task. This example goes for all of the repair work in your home. This is just one small example of to attempt to get the point across of a poor estimate versus an accurate estimate. If we take a stand-up shower as an example, then the estimate would need to account for the pan, drain, floor tile, and mortar bed. However, this is just the wall tile. It is a massive amount of information to absorb, and we are not trying to teach you estimating. This is just to emphasize how crucial it is to have an accurate estimate to ensure you are fairly compensated for the repairs needed in your home.

Scenario 3

Third, going back to the example above of 3 damaged bullnose and 1 tile, let's say you and your adjustor decide that you just want to replace the three pieces of bullnose and a couple of pieces of tile, which will be matched as best as possible. That's fine, but remember, you're owed for the entire shower. If you have a knowledgeable adjuster, they will put in for the replacement of the whole shower because you are owed for it. The adjustor will depreciate it, so it's your choice whether or not you want to live with the mismatched tile. But at least you're being paid for the value of what you're owed. That's why you have depreciation. This goes to remembering you filed a claim, and if you file the claim, you definitely want to be paid for everything that you're owed. You don't get a break for using less. Rates will still go up.

Let us add to what was just said, and let's say you told your adjuster that you are just looking for the tile to be replaced where it was removed. You're trying to be honest and not take advantage of the situation but instead, your adjuster will. The adjuster **should** know you are owed for the whole shower, but since you said you could just replace the missing tile, you will only get a tile minimum, which the adjuster will be happy to do because now it will only be a small fraction of the cost of what you're actually owed. Then, months later, when your rates go up or you get dropped, you will realize your carrier does not care.

They typically aim to minimize the payout for your claim. This is supported by tens of thousands of estimates, and in my experience, carriers rarely pay the full amount owed. It often becomes a negotiation process, especially if you have an experienced estimator advocating for you. REMEMBER THAT!!!

This is the main focus of how insureds get underpaid for their repairs. The accuracy of the estimate and the quality of repairs depend largely on the person writing it and their experience. However, you may not know this until your loss is negotiated or you are faced with a future claim. Therefore, it's essential to read and understand these aspects beforehand to be adequately prepared.

The insurance carrier would love not to pay what is owed; however, is it really the carrier? Or the adjuster who is not properly trained? The fact is you can have numerous issues with one adjuster, but it will be different with another adjuster from the same carrier if they have better training and background. There are no two adjusters alike. So, it's two-fold. It comes down to the adjuster, who does not want to be told how to do the task but rather they tell you. You will see this a few times in this book that adjusters' egos, pride, and arrogance is what starts the problem; however, if they were properly trained by the carrier, this would be less of an issue. Yet, think about this: if the majority of the claims get underpaid because homeowners do not have the proper knowledge, then why bother training the adjuster properly at all.

Appraisal

Appraisal will be discussed in more detail later on. This is just to inform you of what you should do if you are faced with having to go to an appraisal or engage in a last-ditch effort. The challenging aspect of insurance claims lies in comprehending coverage and its application. In essence, your contractor and adjuster can be right. The irony is quite thick when it comes to insurance. For a simple example, what if you're going to go to an appraisal about the difference in floor sanding? Your contractor is adamant that two additional rooms need to be sanded, but your insurance adjuster objected. You should really be getting that answer as to why from your adjuster. Their objection might be because of how coverage is applied. Your contractor sees all the same color floors; therefore, all floors should be sanded, right? No, they would be wrong if there is a break in the floor, such as a saddle/threshold. However, let's get creative and use a real-life argument. There was no break in the floor, but the adjuster objected because the floor changed direction when going into the other rooms. Now, this would be wrong on the adjuster's side. You are entitled to compensation for the **uninterrupted** application of polyurethane on the floor. A flooring installer is unlikely to provide a warranty for their work if it is not executed correctly. Before engaging in any discussion about appraisal, it is advisable to thoroughly review and address any existing differences or discrepancies beforehand. This further goes into policy language of matching undamaged areas if that is a part of your personal policy. In some states, there is a matching of undamaged property buried deep in the policy, which puts a cap on how much you will receive. It is usually a percentage of your policy limit.

Additionally, it's important to remember that the process of going to appraisal can incur costs ranging from $1000 to $3000, depending on the size of the loss. Therefore, unless a substantial disagreement warrants such expenses, it is advisable to carefully reconsider the decision to pursue an appraisal.

Once all discussions and negotiations have reached an impasse, and you and your contractor/estimator are confident that you are being underpaid, the next step is to inform your insurance adjuster. If there is no further flexibility, you have no alternative but to file a complaint with the Department of Financial Services (DFS). Additionally, make it clear that in the event that the resolution favors your position and it is determined that the adjuster was in error, you reserve the right to file another complaint with the Department of Financial Services (DFS), highlighting concerns of incompetence on their part. Kindly request reconsideration within the next two days, emphasizing that failure to do so will result in filing a formal complaint. Upon reaching the specified timeline, proceed to file the complaint with the Department of Financial Services (DFS). Clearly articulate your issue and emphasize the unfairness of having to bear out-of-pocket expenses due to their perceived inexperience or mishandling. Provide a detailed account of the problem for the DFS to investigate.

Demand for the appraisal process in writing. Following a favorable outcome in the appraisal, follow up with a complaint to the DFS, reinforcing the validity and merit of your initial complaint. While it may not directly benefit you, it serves the purpose of preventing a similar situation for future insured individuals dealing with the same adjuster. Additionally, when the adjuster is up for license renewal, your complaints can potentially have a bearing on the decision to renew, highlighting the importance of proper training and adherence to standards. This underscores the significance of reserving the right to further complaints, shedding light on whether the adjuster genuinely believed in their position or if there were deficiencies in their training by the carrier.

Appraisal Explained

What is an appraisal?

When faced with a situation where both the insurance adjuster and the contractor are unwilling to alter their estimates/scope, the final option is to pursue an appraisal. The homeowner must formally demand the requested appraisal in writing.

In essence, an appraisal involves setting aside the existing estimates and obtaining fresh perspectives by appointing two new individuals/appraisers—one for the insurance company and one for the homeowner. The homeowner is responsible for selecting and paying for their appraiser, a cost that is not reimbursed. Simultaneously, the insurance company will choose and cover the expenses of its own appraiser. Once the appraisal demand is accepted, the process begins, with an umpire selected to review the conclusions/estimates of the two appraisers. If the umpire reaches a final decision, it is binding. Although litigation remains an option, it can be a costly endeavor with uncertain outcomes.

The insurance company will choose its appraiser. If there are objections to the chosen individual/appraiser then there will be a presentation of alternatives. Following the selection of appraisers, a meeting is scheduled for an on-site inspection where both appraisers review the project and go over the entire scope of work. The duration of this process varies, being relatively quick for smaller losses but potentially taking days or weeks for significant losses. The appraisal process represents the homeowner's or public adjuster's last resort.

To summarize, the key players in the appraisal process are the homeowner's appraiser, the insurance company's appraiser, and the umpire overseeing the appraisal.

Choosing the right appraiser is crucial, as their competence ensures the accuracy of the written work in relation to the original repair specifications. Mere claims of being an appraiser do not guarantee knowledge of all construction aspects, given the complexity of the industry where one facet affects another. Opting for appraisal should be a last resort, as the cost and time involved detract from the actual repairs. Before proceeding, it is essential to thoroughly explore all available options.

Before initiating the appraisal process, homeowners should evaluate whether their adjuster fulfilled the fiduciary responsibility and acted according to the home insurance policy. If dissatisfaction arises, filing a complaint with the Department of Financial Services, which regulates the industry, can potentially intervene and prevent the need for appraisal. The industry is often marred by inexperience and incompetence among adjusters, emphasizing the importance of engaging experienced remediation contractors familiar with the intricacies of the field rather than relying solely on traditional contractors. The disparities in cost often stem from missing scope elements, highlighting the need for a comprehensive and accurate estimate that aligns with the insurance company's breakdown.

Department of Financial Services (DFS)

The Department of Financial Services, known as the DFS, functions as a regulatory body in each state, overseeing and managing the insurance industry. It serves as a vital resource. If your adjuster fails to fulfil their responsibilities, it is possible to file a complaint against the company. However, filing a complaint against the adjuster's license holds more weight, as they are more concerned about safeguarding their professional standing. To illustrate, for a lawyer, receiving a call from the bar is the equivalent of the DFS contacting an adjuster.

I am a Public Adjuster, and I want to clarify that you don't necessarily need these services to handle matters with your insurance company. While hiring a Public Adjuster can be advantageous for complex projects or coverage issues, in simpler cases, it may just lead to unnecessary expenses that could be better utilized for your home repairs.

Let me commence by delineating the procedure. Public Adjusters do not typically reveal the details I'm about to disclose, as they illuminate facets they prefer to keep concealed. For Instance: In an unfortunate incident like a fire, once the safety of your loved ones is assured, it is crucial to promptly notify your insurance company. By "immediately," I mean that while the fire trucks are still on the scene, you should already be placing a call to your insurance company. Keep in mind that within a 500-foot radius in any direction of those fire trucks, there is a flurry of Public Adjusters and insurance company vendors eager to gain your attention. In some towns, they are prohibited from approaching you until all first responders have left the scene. Unfortunately, this is not the case in most areas. These individuals will attempt to capitalize on your distress, anxiety, misfortune, and your uncertainty about what to do. They will exploit these emotions to persuade you to sign a contract with them while you are under duress. They claim to know how to handle your insurance company, asserting that the carrier will attempt to disadvantage you in terms of coverage. They assert that they are the best choice for your current situation. Even if you manage to avoid signing a contract at this stage, you will likely receive calls on your cell phone from unfamiliar individuals attempting the same. In all the circumstances I have just mentioned, I strongly advise against signing a contract with anyone without making an informed decision. The only scenario in which you truly need a Public Adjuster is if you encounter problems with your carrier regarding coverage or face difficulties with them. While Public Adjusters often portray carriers as problematic, the reality is quite the opposite. Carriers typically provide a repair scope, most likely from a builder they have hired. However, the competency of this scope may be questionable, and certain details may be omitted. This is why it is essential to hire an estimator who is familiar with how insurance companies draft their estimates. Regrettably, acquiring the services of an estimator presents challenges, as engaging one typically involves contacting a contractor. The subsequent steps in this process can lead to various outcomes. Initially, it's likely that the contractor will refrain from providing an estimate unless a contractual agreement is established for the entire project.

Such contracts often include clauses stipulating that cancellation will incur charges for the estimate.

Consequently, if your intention is solely to obtain an estimate, this could become a costly endeavor. While everything comes with a price and value, many contractors impose a fee of around 10% of the total amount sanctioned by the insurance carrier. In comparison, a Public Adjuster would have charged a similar fee, making their services potentially more beneficial in this scenario.

Relying on the proficiency of the person creating the estimate introduces a common challenge across the industry. The quality of an estimate often hinges on the estimator's expertise, and their familiarity with specific tasks, such as drywall and painting, may not necessarily extend to other areas like finish carpentry or electrical work. Consequently, there is a risk of overlooking essential components of the scope, and this oversight may go unnoticed. The accurate determination of scope is paramount in the claims process, impacting the financial aspect of repairs. Without a comprehensive understanding of what can be billed or the items that merit charges, there's a potential financial loss in the repair process.

Deciding whether to pursue appraisal for a reevaluation of estimates also places reliance on the experience of the individual crafting the estimate. Achieving accuracy in the initial estimation is crucial, as the reevaluation process may lead to the same challenge of individual expertise. The presentation of the estimate requires a nuanced approach, considering that each individual may respond differently. Drawing on our extensive experience, which encompasses not only managing construction but physically doing the work in all phases of the construction process, we have refined our expertise over 35 years in the construction field and 25 years in the insurance industry. This cumulative experience assures a high level of confidence that we seldom overlook any components within the scope owed to the insured during a loss.

Keep in mind that opting for a Public Adjuster is all about convenience. It involves more than assigning a monetary value from the outset; you must substantiate the figure and negotiate. In my experience, a significant number of Public Adjusters tend to exaggerate claims, an unprofessional practice aimed at securing higher payouts. However, if you diligently prepare a repair estimate, there's no need for such embellishments to obtain the necessary funds. This information provides an experience where investing time and effort in researching and educating yourself becomes worthwhile. This way, you can make informed decisions that best suit you and your family.

What is a Public Adjuster (PA)?

A public adjuster represents the homeowner or insured, which is you. They serve as the primary liaison with the insurance carrier, alleviating you from the need to interact directly with them. The public adjuster is responsible for coordinating with the insurance provider on your behalf. They may suggest and oversee contractors to carry out the required tasks for restoring your home or completing necessary repairs. Additionally, a public adjuster meticulously examines all relevant documentation related to the claim and engages in negotiations to come to an agreement. This includes additional living expenses or ALE, contents inventory for value, packing-out and packing-in of contents, negotiating the depreciation for contents and/or building repairs, loss of rent, and business interruption. The public adjuster will charge a fee for these services that can vary in range and also have to do with the size of the claim. This charge can go as high as 20% in some states. The average fee is between 8% if the claim is large meaning over $250K to 12% for anything lower.

The challenge with this fee lies in its impact on your repair budget, presenting a significant drawback to hiring a public adjuster. This service fee is **deducted** from your repair funds. Depending on the specifics you contracted the public adjuster to do, it may also be drawn from your mitigation, asbestos, or inventory/contents. For losses under $50,000, you can anticipate the maximum percentage fee applicable in your state.

Public Adjustor Fees

This is how their fee structure operates:

Most public adjusters, if not all, aren't contractors themselves. Instead, they engage contracting companies to draft repair estimates. A portion of the fee you're charged is allocated to compensate this contractor for their estimate as well as paying fees to other contractors relative to the claim. Subsequently, that same contractor may approach you to carry out the repairs. This situation can either be advantageous or turn into a significant challenge. It is crucial that your public adjuster considers the professionalism and quality of work when dispatching a contractor to assess your house. However, since public adjusters primarily aim to obtain an estimate, they might not always prioritize these factors.

Consequently, hiring the recommended contractor may lead to unforeseen issues such as delays, untidiness, failure to adhere to schedules, and cutting corners. The list of potential problems can extend, emphasizing the importance of thorough research and vetting before selecting a contractor to work in your home. Once you're in a contract with an unsatisfactory individual, it can be challenging to terminate the agreement, adding more stress to an already difficult situation.

Additional fees that raise concerns and may be considered unprofessional are referral fees. Your public adjuster might have been recommended by a friend, colleague, or someone you've crossed paths with. Alternatively, they could have been suggested by someone with prior experience using that public adjuster. Typically, these referrals involve a fee, either in cash or checks, as those making the recommendations aim to continue generating business. Fortunately, the Department of Financial Services is increasingly regulating how referral fees, or kickbacks, are managed.

While giving a positive reference is acceptable, receiving a fee for endorsing someone with a negative track record is both unethical and immoral. This practice will likely persist until a more effective regulatory system is established, as it is a common aspect of business operations. Unfortunately, if the contractors working on your project were recommended by your public adjuster, there might also be a kickback going back to the adjuster. This intricate web of referral transactions turns a claim into dirty business tactics instead of hiring the best team to complete your repairs.

Ideally, referral services should operate on a reciprocal basis—meaning, you refer work to me, and I refer work to you. In this model, money is not supposed to exchange hands as such, financial incentives can lead to biased and unfavorable referrals.

What does a Public Adjuster do?

When a PA is dealing with an insurance adjuster, typically, a PA will bring in their contractor/builder to write the estimate for the repairs. Once those estimates are completed, they will forward them to the insurance adjuster. The adjuster will either do one of three things.

1) they have already written their estimate,

2) they have their own builder/contractor estimate or

3) they will write their estimate of the PA's estimate sent to them, reducing certain scope to make it look like they're doing their due diligence. If your public adjuster has a good estimator, knows what they're doing, and knows all aspects of construction, this is the best-case scenario. It will work in your favor since everything was done properly. The estimate gets returned by the adjuster with their numbers, which are always going to be lower than those of your contractors. That is where you have a roundabout idea of what the amount of the loss is going to be approved or finalized. Sometimes, there's not that much of a difference, and it is just agreed to split the difference. Checks get cut, and the repair process begins.

In significant losses, the adjuster may collaborate with a builder to draft a comprehensive scope of work alongside the public adjuster's estimator. Mutual agreement on the scope is essential, and the way the estimate is structured holds paramount importance. Negotiations follow, with both parties settling on a figure that is then approved by the adjuster, facilitating the issuance of checks for repairs.

There is another type of adjuster, which is an Independent Adjuster or IA. They act as the principal for the carrier. The loss comes to the IA as an assignment. Essentially, the IA will settle the claim even though they don't work directly for the insurance carrier. The difference is that independent adjusters have relationships with certain estimators, public adjusters, carriers, and how they articulate their

business with each one of them can be different. There is nothing carved in stone about how they run and operate their businesses. Just to operate with moral ethics and adhere to the policy language within your policy. With that being said, certain individuals will get more of a break or easier approval than other adjusters. In other words, each IA has its own personal relationships that affect the outcome.

However, this would never be an issue if adjusters were trained more efficiently to do their jobs. As a result, independent adjusters may inflate their estimates significantly, reaching an excessively high figure simply because they lack the ability to justify the necessary work accurately.

In response, public adjusters adopt a strategic approach by refraining from submitting their estimates to independent adjusters immediately. Instead, they wait for the independent adjuster's estimate and then compare it to their contractor's figure. If their contractor's estimate is lower, the public adjuster engages their contractor to scrutinize the independent adjuster's estimate for opportunities to raise the overall estimate. This means they find items they missed and place them into their estimate, raising the estimate higher.

This allows them to submit a higher estimate than the IA's. Then, negotiate a final figure that falls between the two estimates or splits the difference. Even when the public adjuster receives their contractor's estimate that surpasses the independent adjuster's estimate, they often instruct their contractor to scrutinize the independent adjuster's assessment. The goal is to identify and incorporate any overlooked details into their estimate, further inflating the final figure. This will give a higher number of interns a higher number for splitting the difference. Let me explain this paragraph in more layman's terms.

Estimating is an art; much like individual painting styles, everyone is unique. Imagine asking two painters to create a mural on a wall with the same theme—while the concept remains consistent, the execution will vary significantly. The dynamic is no different in the realm of insurance claims, particularly when dealing with Independent Adjusters (IA) and a Public Adjusters' (PA) contractor.

When an Independent Adjuster provides an estimate that surpasses the PA's contractor's initial assessment. The PA tasks their contractor with scrutinizing the IA's estimate, looking for items they missed, and then adding them to theirs. These additional items solidify their stance and prevent any later rescinding of these agreed tasks. The result? An estimate that is now higher than the Independents Adjusters estimate.

Conversely, should the contractor's estimate exceed that of the Independent Adjuster, the contractor meticulously reviews the IA's estimate for discrepancies. Identifying these disparities, they add to their estimate accordingly, not only aligning with the IA but also increasing their own figure. For instance, if the PA's contractor originally specified servicing a hot water heater, and the IA estimated for replacement, then the contractor revises their estimate to reflect this change. Essentially, both parties agree on the same line items, contributing to a larger estimate, yielding a higher number if splitting the difference. The above scenarios also apply if no Independent Adjuster is assigned and the insurance adjuster/carrier building consultant writes the estimates.

While this practice may benefit both the public adjuster and the homeowner, it is ethically questionable. Such actions contribute to the challenges faced by the insurance industry, which is grappling with financial misinformation and struggling to maintain stability within states, often leading to potential exits. The realm of claim handling is rife with various forms of misconduct; the amount of reasonable regulation can only go so far, and therefore, it is considered controlled chaos within the industry.

Why would you want a Public Adjuster?

A public adjuster is there to represent you in the complexities of an insurance claim, which can be incredibly intricate and stressful. By enlisting a public adjuster, you can ease the burden of navigating through these complexities. However, it's essential to note that in exchange for their services, you'll need to relinquish a portion of your compensation from the insurance carrier. You are agreeing to spend less money on repairs for convenience.

In situations where your schedule is exceptionally hectic, and you prefer a streamlined resolution without personal involvement, hiring a public adjuster becomes a practical choice. On the other hand, if you're inclined to invest time in understanding the intricacies of insurance, you may find that, despite its complexity, managing the process independently is feasible.

Drawing from my experience as a public adjuster, I suggest hiring a PA as a last resort. While public adjusters may initially promise significant results, they often fall short, leaving you dissatisfied. It's crucial to weigh the convenience they offer against potential drawbacks, such as financial motivations that might not align with your best interests and overall less money for repairs.

Why you need a Public Adjuster?

Let's discuss situations in which you might find it necessary to enlist the services of a public adjuster. If you encounter challenges in securing coverage for a claim and face denial, a public adjuster can be

instrumental in reversing that decision. They possess a deep understanding of insurance policies and can navigate the intricate language within your personal policy, making them particularly valuable in such circumstances. Another scenario warranting the involvement of a public adjuster is when you experience difficulties with your insurance carrier. This could include issues like non-payment for specific aspects of your claim, unfair treatment, lack of communication, or delays in processing your claim.

When considering the hiring of a public adjuster, it is crucial to conduct thorough vetting. Seek referrals and check references to ensure their credibility. It's important to remember that public adjusters receive a percentage of your claim, and in some cases, they may recommend an appraisal. Keep in mind that the cost of the appraisal, typically ranging from $1000 to $3000 depending on the size and complexity of the loss, is paid directly by the homeowner. Additionally, the appraisal process will extend the time it takes to settle the claim by an extra month. Therefore, a careful evaluation of your specific needs and the potential costs involved is essential before engaging the services of a public adjuster.

Why you don't need a Public Adjuster?

Based on 25 years of experience in the insurance industry, it's evident that Public Adjusters often prioritize their own interests. The information here is crafted to empower you to handle the process independently. Hiring a Public Adjuster becomes necessary only when issues arise with your insurance carrier. Meaning the carrier becomes difficult. They can also speak utilizing the language of your policy. This your contractor/estimator is **NOT** allowed to do unless they posse an adjuster's license or they are a lawyer. They prove valuable in expediting a delayed process or if you're dissatisfied with the amount estimated by the insurance adjuster. While the goal is fair compensation without external help, the reality often falls short. Employing a Public Adjuster doesn't guarantee more money; it merely relieves you of the stress of managing the claim yourself. In the end, the payout hinges on your contractor/estimators estimate, and Public Adjusters lack the expertise to determine the true extent of owed tasks, thus relying on the contractor's figures. Ultimately, they can elevate the amount, yet pursuing the claim independently on your own initially might yield a comparable outcome.

Here is an important item to remember. If you are patient, you can always wait for your carrier's adjuster to send over an estimate for your approval. You then can then review it or take it to your contractor and see if you are being paid fairly. If not, then hire a PA to step in. Most insureds don't know that this is the best way to make an informed decision without the use of a PA. You will be led to believe that your carrier is incompetent and will not pay you a fair and reasonable amount for your claim, but that is not always the case. Remember the state that you live in. In some states, a PA's fee is in addition to what is negotiated for the claim. In most states it will be reduced from the amount you receive. Putting that into perspective, if you have a $50, 0000 claim, 10 to 20 per cent of that will go to the Public Adjuster. It may not seem much. However if you have a high deductible, it will play a major part in the decision. If you hire a PA right at the beginning, you will not be able to make that decision. It is very difficult to take this into consideration at the time of a claim. Stress and anxiety will be taken advantage of as you are very overwhelmed. That is the reason for the initial aggressiveness made by PAs and vendors (carrier contractors) & non-venders (independent contractors) to sign with them initially. So, the investment in this information is more valuable to you then signing with a Public Adjuster.

Public Adjuster Summary

The rationale for not hiring a Public Adjuster is self-evident because you don't need one .You can thoroughly review the information in this book and independently manage all necessary tasks or empower oneself with the tools to oversee the contractor and their estimates.

Here is the short list of addressing a claim. Upon hanging up the phone for filing the initial claim, a mitigation company to begin is likely already resolved unless it is a fire. An authorization or proceeds contract will be signed with whatever mitigation company you go with, and the insurance company will be billed for the mitigation costs. If the mitigation company is a non-vender and they are dissatisfied with the insurance payment, you may receive an invoice for the difference your carrier did not pay. It's crucial to identify who you are signing with to prevent any property liens if the insurance payment falls short. Most mitigation companies generally accept the insurance payout without pursuing homeowners for additional amounts due to the potential negative impact of social media reviews.

Your insurance company will recommend a vendor, or you might have your own remediation contractor. Allow them to handle the estimates and negotiations for repairs. In cases of disagreement during the estimating process, consider the appraisal process or file a complaint with the DFS for ethical concerns. Once completed, you can choose to hire the contractor who wrote the estimate or breach the contract and engage your own contractor. If unexpected issues arise during repairs, inform your insurance company promptly, document and photograph as a **supplement**, and allow them time to inspect. Failure to permit inspection may jeopardize reimbursement due to policy violations.

Understanding these processes eliminates the need for a public adjuster (PA), and alternative avenues exist for resolving claims at a fair and reasonable cost. This information provides insights that neither a PA nor a remediation contractor wants you to know. However, remember that providing finished photos of completed work is essential to receiving depreciation, and you must incur the depreciation costs. We are here to help you get through your claim.

Insurance Claims & Contractor Selection:

A Complete Guide

What is a vendor?

In the insurance realm, a vendor refers to a company endorsed and sanctioned by the insurance carrier. These entities possess the necessary qualifications to generate estimates and carry out the tasks required to restore your home to its pre-loss state. They collaborate with the insurance company to determine a fair and reasonable cost for reinstating your property to its original condition. Opting for a vendor often streamlines the process for homeowners, ensuring the efficient completion of work. However, this choice may forfeit the freedom to select your own contractor.

The advantages of employing a vendor include the seamless execution of work within a reasonable timeframe, provided the vendor is proficient. Despite these benefits, based on experience, it may not be the optimal choice. Utilizing a vendor raises questions about whether you are genuinely receiving the full compensation owed for the loss. From my perspective, a conflict of interest arises when writing for an insurance company aiming to minimize costs for the necessary work. Additionally, the outcome depends on which party reaches the project first.

A vendor aims to promptly document losses, facilitating the writing of repairs for timely submission to the insurance adjuster. The insurance adjuster then evaluates the document, makes reductions, and approves the scope of work. However, if the adjuster independently wrote an estimate before the vendor, discrepancies in scope or cost can arise, posing a challenge for the vendor in maintaining a positive working relationship.

When the vendor's estimate significantly differs from the insurance adjusters, amounting to potential tension, the vendor must delicately explain the variations without jeopardizing their standing with the adjuster. This delicate communication is crucial as upsetting the adjuster could lead to a loss of future work opportunities. In instances where the vendor's estimate is higher, they may strategically present a more palatable figure to align with the adjuster's expectations, often lower than the original amount.

This process can be challenging, especially since homeowners may be unaware of the intricacies involved in estimating costs. Consequently, they remain unaware of any compromises made by the vendor to bridge the gap in cost, potentially resulting in corners being cut to maintain profitability. While some vendors may succumb to such pressures, it's important to note that not all engage in this practice.

Corners end up getting cut because some vendors are incentivized to maximize their margins, leading to compromises in work quality, a common practice in the industry. So, to put it more simply, if your adjuster is at $10,000 & the vendor is at $18,000, they may agree to $15,000; however, due to incentive programs, there is an incentive to make that difference up by cutting quality in order to keep better margins so the project manager running your job profits from that.

In my experience working for a vendor, I have witnessed colleagues succumbing to these pressures due to incentive programs that reward favourable margins at the year-end. Homeowners must choose vendors with integrity and transparency to ensure that corners aren't sacrificed for financial gains.

A pro to using a vendor grants leverage to the homeowner. The contractor wants to avoid complaints to the adjuster. Having a complaint can jeopardize future work from the adjuster. So, if it comes with the risk of potential corners being cut, just let the vendor know you will call the adjuster and make a complaint. Unfortunately, this happens more often than you would think. Insureds are typically not aware that they can complain to the adjuster who recommended them in the first place.

What is a non-vendor?

In the broader context, a non-vendor emerges as the preferred choice of contractor for homeowners. Unlike vendors, non-vendors operate without conflicts of interest with insurance carriers and prioritize the homeowner's best interests. They are not concerned with appeasing adjusters and are willing to stand firm in negotiations, even if it means challenging the adjuster's decisions. Prioritizing the homeowner's needs, non-vendors can offer a more transparent and unbiased assessment of repair costs.

Before choosing a non-vendor, it's crucial to conduct thorough vetting. Similar to vendors, non-vendors may include breach of contract clauses, often charging fees if homeowners decide against proceeding with their services. Despite potential fees, opting for a non-vendor can be more financially advantageous for larger losses, as their fees may be fixed rather than a percentage of the overall repair cost.

Ultimately, the choice between a vendor and a non-vendor hinges on the competency and experience of the estimator or contractor involved. The negotiation process between the adjuster and the non-vendor requires justifying the scope of work emphasizing the importance of the estimator's construction knowledge. This negotiation phase may involve reaching a compromise or, in extreme cases, pursuing legal avenues such as filing complaints or demanding appraisal. Put more simply, you will constantly hear "that it's just a number they're trying to get to," which is not true initially. The scope of work needs to be justified in accordance with your policy. Once that's done and the scope is correct, it becomes just a number between the adjuster and the contractor.

More simply put:

This implies that simply stating it's a $35,000 loss isn't enough; the adjuster may assess it as a $25,000 loss. In common scenarios, when there's a $35,000 estimate from the non-vendor and a $25,000 assessment from the adjuster, they often reach a compromise. However, in my experience, the figures aren't usually that close. The non-vendor might propose $35,000, but the carrier often sticks to around $15,000. It's not just a matter of splitting the difference; it involves a thorough negotiation between the adjuster and the non-vendor/estimator to find common ground. This situation requires the estimator/contractor's expertise to **justify the scope of work**. If the carrier and contractor/estimator stand firm without reaching an agreement, options such as initiating an appraisal or filing a complaint with the **DFS (Dept. of Financial Services)** for neglecting fiduciary responsibility and reducing the scope may be considered.

Contract Tactics:

Leading You to Unfavorable Agreements

Public Adjusters tactics:

These individuals will attempt to capitalize on your distress, anxiety, misfortune, and your uncertainty about what to do. They will exploit these emotions to persuade you to sign a contract with them while you are under duress. They claim to know how to handle your insurance company, asserting that the carrier will attempt to disadvantage you in terms of coverage.

They assert that they are the best choice for your current situation. Even if you manage to avoid signing a contract at this stage, you will likely receive calls on your cell phone from unfamiliar individuals attempting the same. In all the circumstances I have just mentioned, I strongly advise **against** signing a contract with anyone without making an informed decision.

Tactics used by the Carrier Contractor who is a vendor:

Insurance carriers carefully evaluate and approve service providers to assess and carry out repairs based on the coverage outlined in your policy. However, potential conflicts of interest may arise depending on the timing of the vendor's presence at your home in relation to the adjuster's visit. It's important to determine whether the vendor arrived before or after the adjuster, as this sequence can impact the objectivity of the assessment. Vendors include construction contractors, content handlers, inventory specialists, and mitigation experts. They are beneficial as they are affiliated with insurance carriers. Nevertheless, it's crucial to keep in mind that these vendors receive business from the same insurance carriers, which could influence the accuracy of their estimates and the scope of work.

The tactic employed involves acting as an intermediary between the insurance carrier and the vendor to negotiate a mutually agreeable price. However, this close relationship sometimes results in a compromise of the scope, and depending on the vendor, corners may be cut to compensate for this compromise.

Non-vender Remediation tactics:

A remediation contractor not affiliated with any carriers is dedicated solely to serving the homeowner/insured. Their primary goal is to diligently address every aspect of the scope, ensuring accurate and policy-covered scope. Possessing a strong comprehension, or dare I say, a superior understanding of justifying their scope, a non-vendor contractor stands out as an optimal choice, free from any conflicts of interest. The non-vendor can hold their ground firmly and refuse to compromise on estimates. They can insist on moving to appraisal, if necessary, without the concern of jeopardizing potential future projects, unlike a vendor. However, the trade-off for this decision is an extended wait for estimate approval. Although the carrier can communicate with the non-vendor, they are not obligated to.

Contractor, do not use for insurance estimate period:

Choosing a non-remediation contractor as the primary decision-maker for your estimate is not advisable. They typically lack experience in the field of insurance and may not comprehend how insurance policies cover claims. If your contractor quotes a price significantly higher than the adjuster's estimate, the adjuster is **unlikely** to approve the higher amount. Even if the contractor's scope of work aligns with the adjuster's estimate, the contractor might struggle to provide a detailed breakdown justifying their numbers. Consequently, the adjuster may only approve the smallest scope, potentially overlooking items you are owed for. While the contractor's estimate may be accurate, without knowledge of the insurance company's program, it's challenging to present a breakdown that aligns with their criteria.

Being Locked Into A Contract

Being obligated to a contractual agreement is a common aspect of hiring services, particularly in the realm of estimates and repairs. It's common for professionals to request a signed authorization or contract outlining their commitment to providing estimates or completing necessary repairs for a fee if there is a breach of contract. This fee is typically 10% or $2500, whichever is greater, and serves as a deterrent to prevent homeowners or insureds from seeking estimates without genuine intent (reminder: DO NOT USE a contractor who has not done insurance work.)

While this contractual arrangement safeguards against misuse, it's crucial to recognize that the 10% fee is akin to what you might pay a public adjuster for similar services. If confronted with such a contract, it might be more advantageous to engage a public adjuster from the outset. As mentioned elsewhere in this book, it's possible to navigate the process independently, but when dealing with a contractor imposing a 10% fee, consider that a public adjuster would charge a similar amount.

Choosing a public adjuster has its benefits, especially when they recommend contractors with whom they have a reciprocal relationship. However, be aware of potential conflicts of interest, as some may receive kickbacks. It's advisable to consider a public adjuster with a license, providing a mechanism for complaints if their services fall short. Notably, terminating a contract with a contractor carrying a fee is relatively straightforward, whereas parting ways with a public adjuster can be more challenging. The decision to hire a public adjuster often means they won't draft your estimate; instead, they may refer a contractor who doesn't charge them a fee. The contractor, in turn, advocates for and justifies the estimate, leveraging their expertise in ways a public adjuster might not.

Why You Should Avoid Hiring a Contractor to Prepare Your Repair Estimate

The insurance industry is a complex puzzle filled with obstacles, loopholes, denials, and coverage nuances that hinge on your policy details. Navigating through these complexities requires expertise in dealing with insurance claims, an area unfamiliar to most contractors. For instance, if your home has wood floor damage in one room but the floor extends into another room with a saddle in between, your policy will not cover that additional room. However, if there is no saddle, then the floors are going to be covered for replacement or refinishing because they are considered continuous. Using the same example a contractor will likely not know how to write for the contents in this room.

Additionally, in that room, the base molding will need to be painted because they will get scuffed up by sanding machines. They may know that in the back of their head but likely will forget to charge for it. They also won't know if your floors have been sanded a few times and that you may be entitled to replace them because the next sanding will wear the life expectancy away. Most remediation contractors don't know that information.

Contractors often lack awareness of matching or non-matching state scenarios. In a matching state, damage to lower cabinets may also entitle you to coverage for upper cabinets. Conversely, in a non-matching state, coverage might extend only to the damaged lower cabinets. Notably, your contractor might not recognize the necessity to detach and reset upper cabinets when replacing lower cabinets—a crucial detail that insurance companies will pay for if included in the estimate.

Insurance companies use programs that break construction projects into individual tasks. Contractors must be adept at breaking down tasks to justify estimates when they exceed adjusters' assessments. This is not a criticism of contractors' abilities but a recognition that estimating is a distinct skill. While contractors excel at executing tasks, many struggle with accurate estimation because it requires a completely different skill set. For accurate repair estimates, it is strongly advised to engage a remediation contractor or estimator experienced in fire and water damage.

Authorization

Insurance companies and your policy form a contractual agreement strictly prohibiting the discussion of policy details with any entity other than those specified in the policy without proper authorization. Granting this authorization empowers your insurance provider to engage with your contractor, facilitating negotiations for a reasonable repair cost. Additionally, it enables your insurer to clarify the coverage details, distinguishing between what is included and excluded.

It is important to note that your contractor cannot speak policy to the insurance company, as they do not have a license to do so. With this granted authorization, most insurance carriers often consider the estimate provided by your contractor to expedite the approval of your repair costs. However, individual preferences vary, and some adjusters may choose not to engage with the contractor, opting to handle the process independently. The authorization can indicate if your adjuster knows what they are doing and can influence the likelihood of resorting to an appraisal or filing a complaint.

Remember, within this authorization is usually the fee that is charged if you breach the authorization/contract. Furthermore, it's essential to understand that authorization is distinct from a contract, which typically outlines the scope of work and details the necessary repairs. Many remediation contractors operate based on insurance proceeds, completing work in accordance with the amount approved by the insurance company to restore your property to its pre-loss condition.

While signing with a contractor without knowledge of their estimate can be challenging, the norm in such situations is to trust in the contractor's expertise and rely on the insurance proceeds to cover the approved work. This arrangement may require you to carefully evaluate and select a contractor who aligns with your comfort level, even though it means committing to an estimate without an upfront price. That is correct. You will be signing an authorization without knowing the price of the work. You can shop around and find companies out there that will write your estimate in the hopes or intent of doing your repairs, yet that can be time-consuming. You need to remember that getting your repair estimate off to the adjuster quickly can only benefit you. If you believe it would be wise to wait and see your adjuster's estimate before comparing it to your contractor's, you would be mistaken. In my 25 years of experience and tens of thousands of estimates, there has never been a case where the adjuster's estimate has been higher. If your contractor's estimate is lower, it suggests you've chosen the wrong contractor. While there may be exceptions, they are rare in my experience.

What is the advantage of getting the estimate off to the carrier quickly?

Adjusters have a very stressful job. They are overloaded and need to get claims resolved. If an estimate is presented to them in their language, meaning written utilizing the insurance industry's program, then more often than not, they will review the estimate. They will make a few minor adjustments and approve. So, getting your repair estimate to the adjuster quickly will only benefit you if you have a **competent estimator/contractor.** There is a lot of Public Adjuster who would disagree with this tactic because they prefer to wait. They aim to increase their estimate further by incorporating additional items not included in their initial assessment. However, in most cases, insurance carriers will not disclose their estimate before reviewing yours. Therefore, disagreeing with this approach can prolong your claim process.

Why do you possess the power?

Possessing an adjuster's license, public adjuster's license or an independent adjuster's license empowers the ability to navigate the intricate language and policies of the insurance realm. Acquiring such a license is no easy feat, given the inherent complexity of the industry. Those who hold these licenses take great pride in the integrity of their individual accomplishments. When dealing with individuals who possess their own hard-earned license, they hold a deep regard for its integrity. In the insurance realm, companies are relatively indifferent to complaints directed at them. In reality, it is the licensed individual who bears the brunt of such grievances, not the company. The license is the individual's property, and any valid complaint jeopardizes their professional standing. Therefore, threatening a complaint against someone's license is not advantageous unless it is genuinely warranted.

This dynamic also underscores why hiring a public adjuster may be unnecessary. If your insurance company's adjuster is not fulfilling their duties ethically or in line with fiduciary responsibilities, lodging a complaint with the regulatory authorities can be a potent tool. The adjuster, aware of the potential impact on their license, is compelled to rectify any lapse in proper procedures.

Every state has a Department of Financial Services that oversees the insurance industry. The last thing anyone desires is a call from them. To illustrate, a lawyer receiving a call from the bar association is similarly unwelcome.

Depreciation

What is AVC VS RCV

Depreciation refers to the reduction in the value of an asset over time. Actual Cash Value (ACV) represents the asset's value at the time of loss, accounting for changes in market value. When an insured item is replaced, the insurance carrier covers the difference between the ACV and the replacement cost, termed Recoverable Cash Value (RCV) or depreciation.

To release the depreciation or RCV, proof of expenditure or completion of the work is essential. Until the policyholder demonstrates that they have incurred the necessary costs, the insurance carrier is not obligated to make the full payment. This process can become costly, especially when a significant amount of depreciation is associated with the loss.

For instance, if a damaged shower is owed for replacement, and the insured initially conveys an intention to replace only part of it, the ACV payout is based on that partial replacement cost. To receive the full RCV, proof of the entire replacement is required, ensuring the insurance carrier compensates for the depreciated amount. Also, given this intention, your adjuster will just write for the replacement of only the area of the damage relying that you will accept this fully, knowing that you are owed for the whole shower. Let us elaborate, as everything you just read is hard to comprehend, so let us use the example from before of the tub tile, but we will go over the entire bathroom and not just the tile. This refers to the **Example of Tub Tile** using **Scenario 1** as the method of estimating.

Real Life Example

In the average home, you'll often find a common bathroom measuring 5’ feet by 8’ feet. Within this space, you'll encounter essential fixtures like a 5’ foot tub, a 3’ foot vanity, and a standard toilet. The tub area spans 2’-8” by 5’-0” with wall tile going to the ceiling. Outside the tub will be floor tile and walls painted to the ceiling. Accessible through a single door, this bathroom also features a medicine cabinet mounted on the wall, complete with a light fixture above.

Phase 1

As you're busy cooking dinner in the kitchen, you suddenly hear the sound of water spraying from the bathroom. Rushing in, you discover water pooling on the floor and streaming from under the vanity. Opening the vanity door, you find that the supply line to the faucet has burst. Acting swiftly, you shut off the valve to stem the water flow, though the entire floor is now drenched. After mopping up, you return to your cooking, planning to call a plumber the next day to address the sink supply line.

The following day, the plumber arrives within hours of your call. However, while downstairs doing laundry, you notice water on the floor and a troubling water stain on the ceiling. Realizing the issue extends beyond the burst pipe, you investigate upstairs to find the vanity swollen from the water, indicating further damage. The plumber fixes the supply line, but upon showing them the ceiling stain, they recommend contacting a mitigation company.

After reaching out, the mitigation company promptly arrives and assesses the damage using infrared and a moisture meter. They reveal that the water has spread behind the vanity, along the back of the toilet, and towards the tub wicking up in the drywall. Concerned about mold growth, they advise immediate action, presenting options for direct payment or filing an insurance claim. Understanding the urgency, you authorize their services and initiate a claim with your insurance carrier.

You file the claim & receive a claim number to reference. The mitigation company gets to work, removing the vanity, toilet, and affected drywall. Unfortunately, the damage extends further, requiring the removal of drywall up to 2 feet up the side of the tub , along with some tiles. They disinfect the exposed studs, set up drying equipment, and return after three days to ensure thorough drying. During this process, they inform you of some floor tiles popping up due to water damage and offer their repair services upon your interest. Upon completion, they obtain your Certificate of Satisfaction and leave your home.

Phase 2

Your adjuster reaches out and schedules an appointment for inspection a few days ahead. Meanwhile, you contact the mitigation company to arrange repairs. We will now call them the contractor. The contractor swiftly arrives, obtains your authorization to communicate with your insurance, and assesses the damages, leaving promptly. They draft an estimate and forward it to your insurer, referencing your claim number and the authorization.

Upon your adjuster's arrival, they review your claim details and opt to write up their own repair assessment. After returning to the office your adjuster writes the repair estimate. The adjuster finds their estimate for bathroom repairs is significantly lower than the contractor's. Your contractor quotes $10,000, while the adjuster's estimate is $5,000. Seeking resolution, the adjuster sends their estimate to settle the loss at $5,000.

The contractor scrutinizes the adjuster's estimate and identifies numerous missing items, resulting in a lower amount. Notably, the adjuster only accounts for minimal tile replacement in the tub , while the contractor insists on a full tile replacement. Moreover, the adjuster overlooks various items like the removing & resetting a small amount of contents and the removal & resetting of the faucet, sink, P-trap, vanity knobs, shower trim, curtain rod, toilet paper holder, towel bar, towel ring, medicine cabinet, and the popping floor tile.

After negotiations, the adjuster agrees to $9,500 with $3,000 in depreciation, mainly affecting the floor and wall tiles. The contractor concurs and too is in agreement with the adjuster.

Phase 3

Before repairs begin you discuss with the contractor to complete all of the necessary work and decide to only replace the three missing bullnose tiles and one single tile, leaving the rest of the tile floor untouched. Your contractor commences with the repairs and when finished, you sign a certificate of satisfaction.

The contractor submits for the release of the $3,000 depreciation, accompanied by final photos. During the review, the adjuster notices the limited tile replacement and the unchanged floor. Consequently, they release the depreciation minus $500 for the shower and another $500 for the floor. Therefore, you receive a depreciation check of only $2,000, emphasizing the importance of thorough repairs to maximize reimbursement.

In conclusion, while avoiding the hassle of a complete bathroom overhaul may seem appealing, depreciation considerations may prompt reconsideration, as incomplete repairs lead to reduced reimbursement. In many cases, the depreciation is intentionally set at a higher rate in such scenarios to deter individuals from profiting from their losses, which is strongly discouraged.

This process can be intricate. If a policyholder decides not to proceed with repairs in a specific area, they will not receive the corresponding depreciation amount unless they provide evidence of completing the work. Different insurance carriers may have varying requirements, some accepting photos as proof, while others demand cancelled checks as evidence of payment to contractors. Understanding the depreciation associated with specific areas of your property is crucial, especially considering that newer components are subject to less depreciation. For example, recent kitchen renovations would likely have minimal or no depreciation if damaged in a covered event.

Supplements

Bear in mind that even if you agree on a scope of work, deposit your check, and commence with the repairs, encountering unforeseen issues should not cause panic. Instead, promptly inform your insurance carrier or adjuster. Allow them time for inspection, or if immediate action is needed, document the situation through photographs and share them with your adjuster. Ensuring the adjuster and carrier are aware of unforeseen circumstances, supported by proper documentation, is crucial. Even if the adjuster doesn't revisit for inspection, notifying them of unforeseen issues during the repair process is essential.

Once repairs are complete, if additional unforeseen problems arise and are documented, you can submit a supplement for the carrier to cover the costs. Consider a scenario where a basement has a quarter-round or cove molding supporting a staple-up 12x12 ceiling or acoustic ceiling tile. If your contractor's estimate mentions replacing the entire ceiling due to the risk of collapse upon removing the molding, and the adjuster omits it, document any subsequent issues. The adjuster may require documentation and photos for a reinspection before approving it as a supplement.

Claim closure is not definite until all repairs are 100% complete within a reasonable timeframe, typically one to two years from the Date Of Loss (DOL), depending on the policy. Supplements play a crucial role in addressing unforeseen situations and protect the insurance carrier from overpayment. If Additional Living Expenses (ALE) are involved, progress in repairs needs to be explained to justify any delays, as ALE expenses can have shorter timelines.

Additional Living Expense (ALE)

Additional Living Expense (ALE) is a part of your coverage D within your insurance policy, addressing the supplementary costs arising from a homeowner's displacement. If circumstances force you to seek alternative accommodation, such as a hotel or another residence, due to your primary dwelling becoming uninhabitable, ALE covers various expenses like food and lodging. Whether you're completely displaced or still residing in your home without a functional kitchen, necessitating frequent dining out, it's crucial to meticulously document all related expenses by keeping track of receipts. This documentation becomes essential for reimbursement with your insurance carrier.

If you were spending, for example, $500 per month on groceries before the

displacement, and due to the situation, your expenses increase to $1500 monthly due to dining out, the insurance company is likely to reimburse you for the difference, approximately $1000. Accurate record-keeping and attention to detail with collecting receipts are necessary in getting reimbursed the money you are owed.

The ALE amount is typically calculated as a percentage of your overall coverage. Still, it's important to note that ALE has a limit, and once exhausted, you are responsible for the additional expenses unless you return to your home promptly. Delays may result in you or your contractor bearing the costs. During your stay in an alternative residence, providing progress reports to your insurance carrier is advisable, offering them an estimate of when you anticipate returning to your primary residence and concluding the ALE coverage. However, if delays are due to alterations or improvements unrelated to the claim, you will not be compensated or allotted more time by your carrier. So be mindful of the changes that will prolong not living in the home.

Tax Grievance

Expanding on the statement above, if you find yourself residing off-site for an extended period exceeding six months and are unable to use your home during this time, it is advisable to consider filing a property tax grievance. Alternatively, you may choose to visit your town hall to discuss the possibility of a property tax reduction, citing the inability to inhabit your residence until necessary repairs are completed.

Properly Written Estimate

A well-crafted estimate resembles a narrative, possessing a coherent beginning, middle, and end. Much like a well-structured story, it should flow seamlessly. When reviewing an estimate, whether from a colleague or contractor, be cautious if it appears disjointed or lacks a smooth progression. A clear, organized estimate is indicative of a meticulous construction process.

The estimation phase plays a pivotal role in the success or failure of any construction project, determining its viability. An estimate should exhibit a logical sequence, starting with detailed elements such as content relocation, detachment, and resetting of various items. It then progresses to rough items like plumbing, HVAC, electrical work, insulation, and drywall, followed by the installation of walls, ceilings, cabinets, trim, finishes, hardware, and finally, floors and cleaning.

A well-structured estimate is a testament to the estimator's understanding of construction processes, showcasing a comprehensive grasp of how elements seamlessly connect. Conversely, a poorly arranged estimate, often encountered with some adjusters, may jump from painting to demolition, flooring installation, back to painting, and then proceed in a seemingly random order. Such an approach suggests a lack of construction background and an inadequate understanding of the logical flow of construction activities. Be mindful that most adjusters write estimates in this manner, and if they lack an understanding of the workflow, they may not be the best choice for creating your repair estimate.

Justifying an Estimates Scope

Justifying the scope is straightforward – it involves firmly grounding yourself and articulating the reasons, purpose, and tasks necessary to complete a specific item. This practice is crucial in detailing the scope of work. For instance, when documenting a replacement of base molding for 24 linear feet, even if the wall extends to 30 feet, the justification lies in specifying only 24 linear feet. Although the intention is to replace the entire 30 feet, it adds weight to the claim by deliberately writing for the lesser amount. This preemptively addresses potential disputes, as an adjuster cannot argue that the linear feet specified do not match the exact missing amount.

This approach applies universally in estimation. Without proficiency in properly articulating and justifying details within the programs utilized by insurance companies, achieving a fair negotiated value is challenging. Demonstrating mastery in justifying the scope allows you to confidently inform an adjuster or carrier that your client is demanding appraisal. It establishes a solid foundation, indicating that your estimates are not arbitrary but thoroughly considered.

In essence, proper justification is about more than merely throwing information at the wall and hoping it sticks. Inexperienced individuals in the field often resort to such tactics due to a lack of understanding in explaining each task. Our expertise stems not only from experience but also from having physically performed these tasks numerous times. Even acknowledging mistakes made decades ago, it is through this wealth of experience that we can thoroughly and convincingly justify every aspect of our estimates. This level of proficiency is what sets apart a contractor facing off against your insurance carrier. These are the qualities you need to inquire and be convinced your contractor or estimator is aware of and can articulate these skills towards your claim.

Devaluing of Kitchen Example

Many instances of water damage primarily affect the lower cabinets, leading to their removal or partial replacement. Replacing damaged cabinets to precisely match the existing ones can pose significant challenges. Additionally, homeowners must be cautious when contractors assert that repairs might devalue the property. Replacing lower cabinets with similar ones may indeed impact the home's value negatively, especially if potential buyers dislike two-toned kitchens.

The discussion extends to scenarios where upper cabinets need replacement, often determined by factors beyond devaluation, such as cabinet condition and age. If upper cabinets are not covered, complications may arise when removing countertops, necessitating backsplash removal and drywall replacement behind the backsplash. Funds allocated for cabinet detachment and resetting could then be redirected towards acquiring new upper cabinets, thereby reducing the cost of replacing the uppers.

Full Kitchen Example

Kitchens are a very expensive task. We will discuss a full kitchen first and address the items that are typically missed in the scope. Instead of explaining the cause of the loss, let's already determine that the entire kitchen is to be replaced, and it has a granite countertop. Most adjusters typically document the linear footage of base cabinets, upper cabinets, and full-height cabinets in their estimates. When you see this in an estimate, you would think that you are getting everything you should be. However, there's more to it with cabinets. Besides the linear feet of cabinets, it's essential to account for additional elements such as crown molding, light rail, roll-out trays, soap-dish trays, lazy Susan, appliance garage, and finish end panels or back panels. These components contribute to the overall scope and cost of the cabinetry project. These additional items are mostly missed on all insurance estimates for kitchens. This needs to be included, or you will have to pay out of pocket for all the remaining details.

However, keep in mind that most remediation contractors, whether vendors or non-vendors are direct dealers for kitchens. Therefore, they are getting them for manufacturer wholesale prices. Whereas if you went to a brand name store and purchased these cabinets, they would be three times the amount. You may have enough money to buy the cabinets but not enough money to install them. So it's very important to remember that with kitchen cabinets, you should be dealing directly with a contractor who is a direct dealer for a kitchen manufacturer. This approach ensures that you are obtaining the most competitive pricing for your cabinets. Many contractors employ this strategy to secure projects and compensate for any potential material cost savings through their labor charges. Insurance companies know most remediation companies are direct dealers for cabinet manufacturers, and it's difficult to argue, except for the individual parts and pieces that they are missing from the above. Typically, your estimator will argue and negotiate this.

Another approach is to obtain three separate independent kitchen cabinet quotes solely for the cabinets from three different stores. This allows you to provide a range of pricing options to your insurance carrier, ensuring transparency and potentially facilitating negotiation for the best value. But they must be exactly what you have in your house, not what you may want to do, but what is actually there. If you get the retail price or list price for those cabinets, the insurance carrier typically will pay for that and pay for the installation of these cabinets separately.

When it comes to a granite countertop, depending on where the seams are, it can be very difficult not to break or damage the countertop when detaching. It can be done, but it does take a professional to do this. The amount of money typically allocated for this task is often insufficient because the task line item assumes the detachment of the countertop with unskilled labor. However, properly detaching materials like granite, quartz, or solid surface countertops requires skilled labor to prevent damage. While technicians during mitigation may handle this frequently and efficiently, ensuring a skilled professional performs the task is essential to avoid any potential damage. If the top is damaged, just document the damage by leaving it in place for you to photograph then let the mitigation crew continue with removing the top. In order to detach a countertop properly and reinstall it properly, your tile backsplash typically needs to be removed. The challenge arises from the presence of 90-degree angles and the difficulty in maneuvering a countertop back into place without risking damage to the backsplash.

Additionally, cabinets that were previously installed may not have been leveled properly, which can exacerbate the issue and further complicate the reinstallation process. When new cabinets go in properly leveled sometimes the countertop will not slide in underneath the existing tile. Therefore, the backsplash typically has to be removed and replaced, which now includes the drywall that is behind it because it, too will be damaged when you remove the tile.

If you are dealing with detaching and resetting a granite/quartz countertop, it is important to note that it is not **detaching & resetting,** which is the line item that is put into the estimate. It is actually **reinstalling** because the seams will now have to be refilled with the same material or color as your existing top as well. You are also owed for buffing and repolishing of that countertop. If the countertop breaks during the process of removal, it needs to be immediately documented, showing where it is in place and where it cracked. As well as informing the insurance adjuster so they have time to come out and reinspect if need be. Most of the time, they will accept the photos. When your countertop is being replaced, also remember it's done by the square foot, so it's a square foot of granite countertop. If there is a cutout for your sink or cooktop stove. You will need to add to the estimate for the cut-out of the sink. If it is a single sink, it is a single basin; if it is a large sink, it is a double basin (also, you cannot detach & reset a sink that's under-mount. It should be in there for replacement.) However, most adjusters will write for detach & reset. If it gets damaged during the detaching, which is common as it's epoxied to the top and breaking, that bond typically damages the top flange or scratches the sink.

The countertop also has an edge that needs to be accounted for. Most countertops for granite have a standard half bullnose/square edge that is included as part of the countertop. Any other edge, such as a backsplash, needs to be accounted for by the linear foot because you will also be charged for it. For instance, if you have a four-inch or six-inch backsplash made of the same material, you need to include that in your measurements and estimates.

When involving the sink cabinet, if the cabinet was installed properly, then it will have small holes thats cut out in the back for your supply lines to run through.

If that is the case, you should be arguing that the valves/stops need to be removed and replaced, as well as detaching & resetting of the P-trap. If a new sink is being installed, there is a strainer that needs to be charged for as well.

Don't forget, if you have under-mount or upper cabinet lighting, you need to account for an electrician to re-snake all this, and that's typically at least four hours of labor. This labor is a lot more meticulous and time-consuming than a typical standard light fixture. There are handles/knobs that are on all the doors and drawers. You are not owed for replacement of those handles/knobs unless it's a fire, so you would need to account for either detaching & resetting every handle/knob or replacing every handle or knob.

When the backsplash goes back on, it's not just tile by the square foot that needs to be accounted for.There are also labor hours that need to be added because the square foot price is not sufficient for installing a tile backsplash. Some estimating programs have a specific line item for tile backsplash installation. Therefore, you would calculate the square footage of the tile and then apply the labor cost based on the corresponding task line item for tile backsplash installation. This ensures that both material and labor costs are accurately reflected in the estimation process. **OR** install by square foot of the tile backsplash, and 2-4 hours' additional time for a tile installer to install the backsplash.

Your appliances should all be in there for detach & reset. If it's an older stove and dishwasher, then a licensed plumber will change the dishwasher connection line and the gas supply line due to safety and warranty. Those items for replacement need to be in your estimate as well.

Partial Kitchen Example

Now, let's discuss the more common scenario where the lower cabinets are damaged, but the upper cabinets are to remain. When it comes to full kitchen replacement, most insurance carriers will inform you that, as per your policy, they only owe for what is damaged. So, if only your lower cabinets are damaged, they'll only compensate for those affected cabinets. Typically, they'll attempt to rebuild the existing cabinets, which can be very challenging if they need to match adjacent cabinets. Over time, wear and tear and ageing will cause the finish to fade, making it difficult to achieve a perfect match. Even if a cabinet company can initially match the color, within six months to two years, the new cabinets may no longer match the originals due to fading. This is a legitimate argument to use when negotiating the replacement of upper cabinets. As cabinets right next to each other will be noticeable and therefore, can lower the value of your kitchen.

Let's maintain a balanced viewpoint. Some homes have never undergone upgrades or improvements, which might not significantly impact the value. Placing an adjuster in such a situation, where their role is to restore your property to its former state, should be approached with a sense of reasonableness. Contesting this could lead to a potentially lengthy appraisal process, potentially with an inexperienced appraiser, which might result in a lower settlement due to the appraisal costs involved.

This brings us to the issue of matching. If you're in a matching state , you're covered. However, if you're not, your only argument may be the devaluation of your home or kitchen, which can be a challenging negotiation. Most carriers will cover at least the lower cabinets, but not necessarily the island if you have one. One commonly overlooked aspect is that the countertop must be removed to install the new cabinets. Typically, this involves removing the tile backsplash, which was installed after the countertop.

Consequently, replacing the backsplash will require properly reinstalling the drywall. To do this correctly, you'll need to detach & reset the entire upper cabinetry, which is often overlooked. In some states, there is a matching of undamaged property buried deep in the policy, which puts a cap on how much you will receive. It is usually a percentage of your policy limit. There is no argument for this language as it is reasonable and prevents an insured from profiting from their loss. However, it also creates an incentive for mitigation companies to remove more materials to ensure they reach another room, thereby circumventing this provision. Consequently, it's advisable not to share your policy details until after mitigation is done when filing a claim. Regardless, mitigation will be necessary whether or not you file a claim.

So even if you're not compensated for replacing the upper cabinets, you may still receive payment for detaching & resetting them. Contractors who are direct dealers with manufacturers often negotiate either free replacement of upper cabinets or charge a small additional fee. However, it's essential to note that the amount allotted for detaching & resetting upper cabinets is typically the same as the cost of the cabinets themselves unless they are premium grade. So even though your carrier is not replacing them, you can use them as a negotiation tactic to get from your contractor.

Regarding the argument that replacing only the lower cabinets may **devalue** your home, it's crucial to have professional backing. This argument may not apply in all cases. Still, a legitimate argument can be made that the replacement of the older upper cabinets is necessary to maintain the value of your kitchen.

When it comes to "like kind and quality," replacing older particle board cabinets with plywood ones may warrant consideration, as most cabinets these days come with plywood boxes. Therefore, the like kind and quality can be used to argue for the replacement of cabinets that are not damaged, as older cabinets are not made with the same material anymore. Every older kitchen is different. So, to use the argument of the new cabinets not being the same is correct, and if you are to replace the lower cabinets with like kind and quality would cost more since the older cabinets are now obsolete can strengthen your argument for replacement. Additionally, the inclusion of maple dovetail drawers in modern cabinets may not align with the like kind and quality when compared to older cabinets since most older cabinets did not have dovetail draws. If they did, they would be a high/premium grade cabinet depending on the age.

Returning to the issue of cabinet fading, if only some upper cabinets are being replaced due to a leak from above and there's a visible window separation with no valance, if the cabinets are being remade to match will likely fade quicker due to sunlight exposure. Consequently, you may have stronger negotiation leverage for the replacement of all your upper cabinets.

Countertops

When it comes to other countertops, like a laminate countertop, it is flat laid. Meaning has a square edge or beveled edge. You need to remember to add or look for a sub-deck underneath it in the estimate. That's how you get the buildup of an inch and a half. It may seem insignificant, but it's still a crucial aspect that often goes overlooked. If you have a post-formed countertop with a rounded edge and a continuous backsplash, there is typically no subdeck present since this type of countertop is pre-made with finished sides adhered with iron-on or contact cement. It's important to consider this in the estimation process. Similarly, when replacing a solid surface countertop, it should also be rebuffed and finished after reinstallation to ensure a proper finish. If it is in for replacement, remember you are not just replacing a solid surface countertop. You're replacing the sink as well. If it is part of the top, and this is a very expensive sink. It’s integral, meaning it’s part of the countertop. Make sure that the sink is a part of the estimate as well as the strainer. Quartz is all the same argument with granite from above.

Kitchen Summary

Now, all this information is very intricate. There are numerous different ways to argue about each small aspect of your kitchen. But the majority of the arguments or problems you are going to come into have been covered for most kitchens above.

Flooring Example

Drawing an analogy to hardwood floors, the impact of repeated sanding on floor life becomes apparent.

If floors have undergone multiple refinishing cycles, they may lose value and require comprehensive replacement. Even after three sanding's, considering the entire floor replacement becomes a viable argument. Homeowners should be mindful of signs, such as base molding irregularities, such as the floor recessing down in front of the base moldings, indicating extensive sanding has been done in the past.

While contractors may initially focus on specific damaged areas, the long-term integrity of the entire floor should be considered to avoid potential issues in matching patches during repairs.

In summary, navigating claims related to water damage involves strategic considerations, and consulting a public adjuster or going to an appraisal can enhance the likelihood of a favorable outcome, especially when addressing complex issues like cabinet and floor replacement.

During negotiations with adjusters, expressing concerns about devaluation may not always yield results. However, involving a public adjuster who understands policy language can prove advantageous. Public Adjusters can assert the obligation to restore the property to its pre-loss condition without diminishing its value. Threatening to file complaints with regulatory bodies or pursuing appraisal processes may be options, though the expertise of a Public Adjuster can streamline these efforts.

Remember, you only need to hire a public adjuster when problems like this arise. However, using the appraisal process may help, but going to the appraisal is a last-ditch effort. **It does cost you your own money to pay for your appraiser, and hiring a public adjuster now obligates you to pay their fee as well.**

These are complicated decisions due to the fact that if your carrier's estimate is $4000 lower, then hiring a Public Adjuster or going to an appraisal may not be the best option because the difference is what you will be paying in a fee to a PA or an appraiser.

Consider this scenario/example.

Consider another common scenario where a main-line blockage in the main sewer line leads to sewage water flooding your bathroom, spreading to the kitchen cabinets on the adjacent wall, infiltrating behind the drywall, and even reaching the hallway and floors. The damage extends to the drywall behind the kitchen cabinets. As a homeowner, you may be apprehensive about a mitigation company tearing out cabinets and flooring. It's advisable not to interfere in such situations. The professionals use moisture meters to confirm water penetration beneath the floors & affecting the cabinets, and they should document that through photos. The water is categorized as level three, and everything it touches must be removed.

However, you still do not want anything in the kitchen removed. So, even after the drying process, moisture readings persist beneath the vinyl floor. Although you may choose not to replace the cabinets, you are owed to have the floors properly removed and the kitchen cabinets, especially the lower ones, replaced. Despite initially opting against cabinet replacement due to construction concerns, circumstances may change. If, six months later, the floor begins to buckle, mold develops, or the damage worsens, you might reconsider and include it in your claim. It's very possible that your carrier will pay for it; however, they may also claim that this is NOT a result of a previous incident, that it could be the dropping of a pot of water, which is why your floor is buckled. Proper documentation is important, so don't lose the chance to be paid for something that you are owed. It's crucial not to miss out on the reimbursement you are owed for, as this will ultimately impact your premiums. Additionally, the insurer might request a new claim, marking your history with two claims instead of one, which will have repercussions for years. Keep this in mind as you navigate the claims process.

So what to take from this example is that if you are owed for something get compensated for it and let the carrier depreciate it. If you never planned on doing the work, that is your choice, but you are still owed for the work.

How to Handle on Your Own

There are various alternatives to explore **without** the necessity of hiring a **Public Adjuster**. You have the flexibility to navigate through different options. As the policyholder responsible for the premium, you hold the authority to select the individuals entering your home unless your insurance company exercises its "**right to repair**", a separate topic entirely.

In the event of a loss/claim, when you engage a mitigation contractor, the mitigation process is typically directly handled/coordinated with the insurance company. The repair estimate is managed either by a vendor appointed by the insurance company, the adjuster, your chosen contractor, or a combination of all three. If you lack a contractor, or unsure about one, or possess a strong background in contracting, let the insurance company present an estimate first. Then, assess the figure for the reasonableness of repairs. Is the cost accurate? If uncertain, involve your contractor or someone knowledgeable for verification. If adjustments are needed, note them down and submit them to your adjuster for consideration. Upon the adjuster's agreement, you have an approved estimate, and any future issues can be addressed through supplements.

If you encounter challenges with your adjuster modifying or decreasing repair values, take specific actions. First, confirm that they are fulfilling their fiduciary responsibility for resolving your claim. If not, notify them of your intention to file a complaint with the **DFS (Department of Financial Services)**. If the issue persists, proceed with filing a complaint. If there's still no resolution, then in writing, demand for appraisal. If handling this independently, you'll need to find your own appraiser, ensuring they align with the scope of work you believe is necessary for your home. Keep in mind that this approach is rooted in policy language and coverage.

Another course of action is to hire a Public Adjuster if you encounter difficulties with your insurance adjuster. However, if the Public Adjuster doesn't make progress, you may need to resort to the appraisal process anyway, incurring additional costs along with the Public Adjuster's fee. These avenues provide control over the situation, potentially avoiding the need to hire a contractor, particularly if you prefer managing the process yourself. In cases with significant depreciation and difficulty proving expenses for repairs, hiring a vendor or non-vendor to document your repairs might be a prudent choice.

Right to Repair

An insurance company's utilization of the right to repair, a provision embedded in policies but was once seldom applied, represents a significant shift. Essentially, the insurer is responsible for coordinating repairs, potentially limiting your freedom to choose the individuals who will be working in your home. This introduces a potential concern as strangers enter your residence, and the specifics of what you are entitled to or not may become obscured, potentially leading to a lack of transparency.

The crux of the matter lies in the insurance policy language, which can be interpreted at the discretion of the company. By invoking the right to repair, the insurer transforms from being merely your insurance provider to also acting as your construction contractor. This transition exposes the insurer to additional liabilities that are typically outside the scope of an insurance company's operations.

While I endorse the concept of the right to repair, my reservation lies in how insurance companies execute it. Many lack a comprehensive understanding of construction processes, placing themselves in precarious positions. Despite my attempts to convey the proper procedures, the insurance industry still remains unresponsive.

Certain states are beginning to witness the implementation of the right to repair, prompting the suggestion that filing a complaint with the Department of Financial Services (DFS) may be a recourse. It's essential to note that the DFS oversees insurance companies and their fiduciary responsibilities but lacks jurisdiction over contractors. Consequently, if the right to repair is invoked, changing your agreement to a construction contract operates outside the regulatory purview of the DFS.

It becomes imperative, under such circumstances, to reject the insurer's invocation of the right to repair. This is due to the absence of oversight mechanisms to ensure proper inspection of repairs and the vetting of hired contractors. Online platforms claiming to verify contractors may lack genuine vetting processes, raising concerns about the credibility of the individuals entering your home.

In conclusion, the insurer's invocation of the right to repair without adherence to proper procedures and policies, especially when transitioning the contractual agreement to a construction contract, poses a significant risk and calls for careful scrutiny and rejection when necessary.

Deeper into Invoking the Right to Repair

Let's delve deeper into the "right to repair" as carriers are starting to implement throughout the country. I have taken the initiative to correspond with CEOs and board members of leading insurance companies, offering comprehensive explanations on how to exercise their "right to repair" accurately. Despite sending ten individual letters to each company, my efforts were disregarded. Invoking the "right to repair" transforms an insurance company's contractual agreement into a construction contract, exposing them to additional liabilities they often prefer to avoid.

However, if executed correctly—beyond mere outsourcing—this shift could slash overall spending by half. Successfully navigating this change would enable insurance companies to maintain or even lower rates, attracting more policyholders. Once an insurance company engages its "right to repair," it operates in a regulatory void. Therefore, if subcontractors or contractors are sent to your home without proper certification, there is a risk of unregulated individuals, possibly with concerning backgrounds, gaining access. It is crucial to exercise caution and consider the qualifications of those entering your home when the "right to repair" is invoked. I don't disagree with subcontracting either; however, I stress that insurance companies, when invoking their "right to repair," must enlist project managers with significant construction backgrounds to guarantee proper oversight of the process.

If Invoking Right to Repair Is Engaged

If you suspect that your carrier is moving forward with invoking their right to repair, it's essential to take measured steps. A letter from your carrier asserting the right to repair does not necessarily mean they will proceed.

If your adjuster confirms their intent to invoke the right to repair, request written documentation of this decision. Additionally, check if this invocation occurs within the initial 30 days from the Date of Loss. If it surpasses this timeframe, question how they can make this decision without taking into consideration they are not living with this problem, you are! There needs to be a reasonable timeline established so you are not left with no completion date.

Should the carrier persist, initiate a complaint with the DFS, highlighting the conflict of interest in the carrier regulating their own repair process and no regulatory oversite from the DFS itself as they too are not contractors. Then, in writing, demand transparency from the carrier, including details about the chosen contractor, their experience, references, employee vetting, and the engineer overseeing the project. That these demands must be provided in writing, not oral, and insist on a letter from an independent engineer/architect confirming the correct completion of the work was done, once work is finished.

Request documentation from the building department regarding the necessity of permits, including a letter confirming a permit is not required and review all paperwork to be submitted. Seek a detailed project schedule, expressing concerns about potential delays due to their contractor juggling multiple jobs. Demand a comprehensive estimate of the repairs, questioning any omissions. Demand for up-to-date insurance on the contractor as well as workers' compensation. Have the contractor list you as additional insured so you are not the victim of an accident involving their own workers. A proper contractor should readily provide this information, even if not invoking the right to repair. If the carrier is taking the choice of your contractor out of your hands, then require all of the insight you would expect from hiring your own contractor.

So let's help you with this so you can just copy and paste the following as most contractors will provide this information if requested. Send this off to your adjuster/carrier and follow through with the demand as they are reasonable.

If your intent is to invoke the right to repair, then I request written documentation of this decision. I understand this is your right to invoke repairs, but just so you know, I will initiate a complaint with the DFS, as this is a conflict of interest, in you, the carrier, regulating your own repair process and no regulatory oversite from the DFS itself as they too are not contractors. Then, in writing, I demand transparency from you, the carrier, including details about the chosen contractor, their experience, and how many times they have done insurance work. I want references, current employee vetting of all and anyone that will come into my home, and the engineer/architect/project manager overseeing & signing off on the project. That these demands must be provided in writing not oral, I will also insist on a letter

from an independent engineer/architect confirming the correct completion of the work. I am also requesting documentation from the building department regarding the necessity of permits, including a letter confirming a permit is not required and reviewing all paperwork to be submitted. I'm also demanding a detailed project schedule, expressing concerns about potential delays due to juggling multiple jobs. I demand a comprehensive estimate of the repairs, questioning any omissions. Demand for up-to-date insurance on the contractor as well as workers' compensation. I demand the contractor list me as additional insured so I'm not the victim of an accident involving their own workers. A proper contractor should readily provide this information, even if not invoking the right to repair. If you are taking the choice of my contractor out of my hands, then I require all of the insight you would expect since my contractor does provide this.

NOW, they will probably respond negatively to this request and send you their letter for the right to repair. It will have wording that they vet high quality professional contractors, you have to execute permits and grant reasonable access to your home. Every carrier has a different letter, but giving you some sort of response and demand to that letter can be difficult. Here is a legitimate response if those are some of the items. Use the following to help respond.

Who exactly has vetted these contractors? What specific procedures were used for vetting, especially considering you aren't licensed contractors yourselves?

While I acknowledge you are paying for damages, it does not grant unilateral authority over my home without transparency on how you're ensuring the integrity of the individuals entering my space. Your vetting process remains unclear. For instance, accreditation with companies that ensure their contractors are the ones to choose from often lacks depth. Most of those online reference companies simply give approval after paying a fee, and providing minimal financials and references hardly suffices, especially in an industry with high

turnover rates for skilled labor. While you may have vetted the company, what about the backgrounds of the workers entering my home? I have established relationships with my own contractors whom I trust. While I'm not insisting on their services, if you're imposing your contractor, you must furnish the information I've requested. Without proof to the contrary, I'm left to wonder if your choice is solely based on cost efficiency.

Regarding permits, it's the contractor's responsibility, not mine. I'm not familiar with the paperwork, as it has always been handled by my contractor in the past. You can't shift this burden onto me while holding me accountable for possible delays in pulling a permit. Pulling permits falls squarely on your contractor, who should also provide proof of a valid contractor's license, not merely operate under another's license. This is a non-negotiable for me.

Cooperation is key, and I'm more than willing to collaborate. My requests are standard for any legitimate

contractor. If you're unable to provide them, it calls into question the legitimacy of the work you're asking me to consent to in my home.

As for a detailed estimate, my contractor has already provided one. I need to see your estimate outlining the scope of work you propose in my home.

You may also get an oral response from the adjuster or, for the carrier, an ultimatum of "If you do not go through our contractor, then you can pay for it yourself." Yes, this does happen and it is to scare you into submitting. The vetting of individuals is lengthy. However, if you are forced into using their contractor, then it is not an absurd request. Any contractor would provide this information to you if they are committed to doing the work.

If that is said to you, please respond with: **"You mentioned that if I don't utilize your services, I can cover the expenses myself. This approach is not just unprofessional but also feels like a form of intimidation. I'm simply making a standard request that any homeowner would make of a contractor. If you're now acting as my contractor, then I'm directing this request to you. Using such tactics to pressure me into using your contractor, warrants a reconsideration. It's concerning when someone who relies on my premiums threaten not only to serve as my insurance provider but also as my general contractor. I intend to lodge a complaint with the DFS."**

Your insurer is prioritizing its financial interests above your needs. However, the insurance industry lacks the capability to enforce the right to repair without proper training. Simply hiring a contractor without competitive bidding for the work is not the appropriate solution. Until this issue is addressed within the industry, it's advisable to resist invoking the right to repair until insurers allow the use of your chosen contractor or their preferred vendor, who can provide the necessary documentation and professionalism expected from all contractors. In reality, carriers will only likely enforce this requirement when they know you're using your own contractor, as they don't invoke it when their vendor is involved, creating a significant conflict of interest.

Experienced Estimator Matters!!!

Distinguishing between adjusters and estimators is crucial. Many adjusters perceive themselves as both contractors and estimators, yet their limitations become evident. A hindrance arises when pride, ego, and arrogance cloud judgment, often stemming from years of experience but lacking the ability to substantiate these qualities. In summary, aligning estimates with actual costs and durations requires practical experience and a commitment to continual learning.

The insurance industry is undeniably intricate and expansive, with numerous facets to navigate. Each trade involved in home-related matters represents an entire industry within itself. Possessing comprehensive knowledge of how these trades intersect and coalesce is exceptionally challenging, particularly demanding seasoned expertise. Unfortunately, finding individuals well-versed in all these fields is a rare occurrence. When crafting estimates, a discerning eye can reveal the strong points of the estimator and a good knowledge of their experience.

What do I mean by different facets & strong points? Let's consider an adjuster with a robust background in painting. Such an individual is likely to possess comprehensive knowledge across various aspects of painting, including expertise in drywall and finish carpentry for door casings, base moldings, and windows. Beyond their proficiency in these areas, they may not be well-versed in identifying additional requirements for a task if the allocated funds fall short. Drawing from their experience as a painter, they understand the time investment required for various tasks.

Let's provide an example for painting a single bedroom. If you see in the estimate the following: Drywall patch on the wall and ceiling, paint the walls & ceiling, and paint the baseboard molding would you know anything other than the insurance carrier is paying for what they owed? Probably not. However, if this were written for real, then you would not have enough money to hire a contractor to do the work.

This would not be enough because the estimate is missing scope. All aspects of a room are broken down in an insurance estimate. The above example is too broad. Besides the above, you are also owed for the following: contents move & reset, blinds detach & reset, prime the patched areas, paint the door openings since the casing is tied to the baseboard molding, detach & reset a ceiling fan if one is in the room, detach & reset any surface mount light fixture, detach & reset any registers, detach & reset recessed light trims, add for carpet/dust protection, detach & reset a outlet or switch if the outlet or switch is in the patch area, detach & reset outlet/switch cover plates, detach & reset shelving. Yes, some of the items mentioned above arc actually in the item of paint, but not all of them. These prep items start to add up after a reasonable amount. This is the difference between an experienced estimator and an incompetent one. Yet, how would you know this unless you were told by someone other than the carrier? There are thousands of examples of this, so if your estimator has a background in painting the above items will most likely all be put in. However, that is just it. Most estimators or adjusters have this one strong facet. Yet, when they estimate for another task like floors or electrical, they will use the same simple line item approach as mentioned above, and you may never know how much more is actually missing from your repair estimate. You really need to get someone who knows what they are doing. This example is also why you see Public Adjusters inflating jobs with unjustified tasks. It is to make up for their inexperience. If you had the right estimator from the very beginning, this would never be an issue. This process can be very overwhelming, but it's here to ensure you make an informed decision.

The insurance carrier's programs are designed to account for insufficient funds by incorporating specific additional elements. The adjuster, drawing on their insights, ensures that all necessary aspects and items are factored in to adequately cover the costs. While this person excels in the realm of painting and related tasks, what about other areas such as insulation, plumbing, electrical work, framing, master carpentry, kitchens, tile, vanities, carpet, plank systems, flooring systems, and hardwood systems?

Although they may possess knowledge of basic line items, their lack of experience in these areas may result in overlooking essential components crucial for a comprehensive repair scope. This underscores the significance of having a proficient estimator who is well-versed in all facets of construction. When dealing with a remediation estimate, it becomes evident that relying on an estimator with a broad skill set is crucial. Without this expertise, there's a risk of overlooking legitimate scope that should be included in the repair plan, and such omissions might go unnoticed. Therefore, having a knowledgeable estimator is essential for a thorough and accurate assessment.

Let's apply the same principle. When an adjuster drafts your estimate, they might have a strong background in one or two trades but lack expertise in others. This discrepancy often results in significant variations between contractors' estimates and those prepared by adjusters. It emphasizes the importance of having an experienced professional who is adept at using the same programs employed by insurance companies. This expertise becomes crucial when justifying why your estimate exceeds theirs.

Effective communication with the adjuster is key. Presenting your reasoning without causing frustration is essential to avoid conflict. In case of disagreements, options include resorting to appraisal or filing a complaint with the Department of Financial Services (DFS) for a breach of fiduciary responsibility. Ideally, the adjuster should send out a vendor to create a comparable estimate. However, similar to the issue with adjusters, the vendor's experience is vital to ensure accuracy.

Public adjusters typically deploy building consultants, but if they lack proficiency in using the required programs, it might not strengthen your case. Some may compensate by simply inflating labor hours, but this approach raises red flags for insurance carriers, as labor hours need justification. The importance of justifying every aspect of an estimate, especially when using bulk items, cannot be overstated. It's crucial to explain and justify any labor hours added to the estimate.

A public adjuster's estimate may appear higher, but it must be justifiable and not merely inflated. The real challenge lies in obtaining approval for unforeseen supplements during the repair process. Insurance companies are unlikely to reevaluate agreed-upon line items, making it essential to get the estimate right initially. Estimators should be fluent in all construction aspects, a quality that might be confirmed through references or a direct conversation.

In summary, even if you have a competent contractor and public adjuster, the estimator's proficiency is paramount. A lack thereof can result in inadequate funds for your project or force compromises in other areas.

Real Life Scenario

Let's delve into real-life scenarios. If I estimate a loss of $100,000, and a public adjuster Builder

estimates the same loss, the Public Adjuster typically will settle within the range of $75,000 to $85,000.

On my end, It will be between $95,000 and $98,000. It's crucial to note that if an adjuster from your insurance carrier handles the same estimate, the figure will be around $65,000 to $75,000 due to the inexperience factor. You will never hear how under-experienced adjusters are. Taking classes and not experiencing real in-the-field construction explains this point.

This isn't to say that all adjusters lack the ability to write accurate estimates; many are proficient. However, they usually prioritize settling the claim rather than having a personal stake in your project. The contractor, on the other hand, has a genuine interest because they're performing the work and understand the associated costs, or at least that's the expectation.

Once an estimate is agreed upon, supplements are possible. However, insurance companies require time to inspect supplements, and failing to adhere to this timeline may result in forfeiting your right to payment unless there is documented communication (email or phone conversation) allowing you to proceed. Continually revisiting the insurance company due to incompetence is unproductive, as they won't pay for the same thing twice. Therefore, precision in the initial estimate is paramount.

Related Real-Life Scenarios

If I write for a $1,000,000 loss, it will settle for around $925,000-$950,000, while the adjuster's builder will come in around $750,00-$850,000, and we will negotiate up to the $925,000-$950,000. Yet, there are some building consultants who work for the carrier/adjuster that will come in just above $500,000. It is that big of a difference. These are simpler to negotiate but usually end up with the builder getting thrown off and a new builder coming out to write for the adjuster. The same thing goes for losses under $50,000. If I write for $35,000, the adjuster can be close or be as far off as writing for $12,000, but in the end, we will settle around $28,000-$32,000. For losses under $10,000, if I write for $10,000 and the adjuster writes for $4000, this becomes an ego/pride thing for the adjuster because a loss of this size is usually handled by a desk adjuster or an adjuster just starting out. Hence, we either settle for no less than $8000, or we will push for appraisal. Most carriers will settle for the

$8,000 provided there is justification for that number and just approve as the cost to go to appraisal will equal that amount. Most losses under $10,000 settle quickly as they are simple, but then again, if the adjuster doesn't want to budge, and yes, that is usually due to ego, pride, or arrogance, it can drag out for weeks or months. This shows you how off the insurance company can be, and this happens most of the time. That is why you really need a great estimator. To avoid this in the very beginning.

Certificate of Satisfaction

Upon the completion of any repair or construction project, it is customary to request the signing of a Certificate of Satisfaction (COS). This document serves as evidence that you are content with the contractor's work and that all contractual obligations have been fulfilled. The same COS is utilized by the contractor when seeking the release of depreciation from the insurance carrier. Alongside conclusive finish photos, the contractor submits the COS to demonstrate the project's completion and request the release of funds. Depending on the insurance carrier, there might be a policy requirement to withhold depreciation until the insured party pays it.

If you're managing the project independently without a contractor, obtaining the release of depreciation becomes more challenging. You must prove payment that all of the money was used to complete your project. Your carrier will ask for proof of this through canceled checks or paid contractor invoices.

In cases where the contractor has financed the entire project, they may request you to sign a Substantial Completion document. This supersedes the COS but includes a list of punch list items, legally binding the contractor to complete the outstanding work. This step initiates the paperwork necessary for funds to be released from the insurance carrier. It's essential to recognize that the last depreciation amount holds leverage over the contractor, as it often represents pure profit. Consequently, the contractor is motivated to address any outstanding items on your punch list to secure the final payment.

Puff back

A puff back occurs when smoke/soot residue is expelled throughout your house. To address this issue, a mitigation company will come in to perform comprehensive cleaning, including wiping down walls, ceilings, and floors. Additionally, they will clean all soft goods within your home. Alternatively, you can opt for a service where a company takes your soft goods offsite for thorough cleaning.

In more severe cases, depending on the amount of soot, the mitigation process may involve painting either specific areas or the entirety of walls and ceilings. The extent of the painting depends on the severity of the puff back. Furthermore, thorough cleaning of ductwork is essential, and if you have flex ductwork, it is advisable to consider its replacement for optimal results.

Inventory

Inventory is done when there are damaged contents, with the process varying based on the scale of damage. For small amounts of damage, adjusters typically handle the inventory during their initial inspection. Larger-scale damage prompts the carrier to engage vendors for on-site inventory. In cases of total loss or significant damage, a crew is scheduled, and your mitigation contractor should provide labor for efficient staging and movement. Setting up tables outside the house speeds up the process, with laborers placing items on tables for photographing & documentation. The valuation will be completed later. If there is any artwork, such as a painting, it will be sent off to a specialist for evaluation. If the paintings can be restored, then the cost of restoring verses the value of the painting itself will be the decider. Obviously, if the painting is of less value than the restoration, then the carrier will only pay for the value. (If you choose to have the painting restored instead, then that is your choice. The same value is also associated with the frame.)

The duration of the inventory process varies based on the extent of contents damage, ranging from a week for smaller losses to potentially months for significant losses. Following completion, the inventory is sent to you for verification, allowing you to cross-check for any overlooked items. Once this review is done, the inventory undergoes an approval process.

Contents are generally compensated on an actual cash basis, and reclaiming depreciation requires proof of repurchase through receipts. Replacement cost value is attained only by repurchasing and validating the amount spent. Without repurchase proof, you receive the depreciated amount. For example, if there's $20,000 in damages depreciated to $12,000, you'll receive $12,000 unless you can provide evidence of repurchasing. However, it's only on the one item that was repurchased.

It's crucial to be aware that once the carrier inventories an item, they become the owners of that item as they are the ones compensating for it. Once the insurance company compensates for the contents, ownership transfers to them, and they may decide to salvage the items. Whether you can keep an item of sentimental value depends on your adjuster's discretion. While most adjusters allow it, some may assert ownership, even for items destined for disposal, and may not compensate you unless the item is released.

Temporary Repairs

Temporary repairs are a critical component of the mitigation process, initiated early on. For instance, in cases of water damage leading to the removal of kitchen cabinets and sinks, a mitigation company installs a temporary sink to allow functionality during the investigation and the entire claims process.

Similarly, broken windows from elements like ice, snow, wind, or rain are promptly boarded up to prevent secondary damages. In large-scale losses such as fires, the entire house may be boarded up to secure it and prevent further damage. Boarding up, tarping, and framing are integral parts of this process. In situations where power is lost, temporary electric is installed in the house. For fire-related cases, an emergency permit facilitates the installation of temporary electrical measures, allowing the electrician to secure the house, reinstall the meter, and energize limited lighting and outlets for mitigation and repair purposes. The comprehensive repair of electrical systems is then undertaken separately under a distinct permit during the repair process. The process may also involve winterizing a home in a cold region if it becomes uninhabitable.

Additionally, introducing heat to initiate the drying process is considered, with the specifics depending on factors such as the building's type, use, and the timing of the loss. The need for temporary repairs can be influenced by various factors.

However, the execution and timing of these processes are often contingent on the coverage in place. Homes that are under-insured or covered by an Actual Cash Value (ACV) policy require careful consideration of how coverage is allocated. It's essential to avoid depleting the coverage upfront and leaving insufficient funds for necessary repairs. Engaging an experienced remediation contractor plays a crucial role in ensuring the effective completion of these processes. This underscores the potential drawbacks of hiring a Public Adjuster (PA) early in the process, as it could impact the strategic use of coverage.

It becomes even more critical to consider the points mentioned above if you do not have any insurance coverage for your home. While this might be unintentional, in cases where you have a mortgage, the bank may impose forced insurance to safeguard their investment. However, it's important to note that this forced insurance is often an Actual Cash Value (ACV) policy, meaning that the funds available are limited.

Consequently, careful planning and strategic allocation of these limited funds become essential to address the necessary repairs and ensure the restoration of your property.

Asbestos

Asbestos is an important consideration for homeowners, particularly if the house was built before 1980. The likelihood of having asbestos is high in such cases. It may exist in non-friable forms like vinyl tiles, particularly 9x9, the mastic it is adhered with, caulking, & roofing or friable forms such as pipe insulation/wrap, transit, plaster, drywall spackle, and shingle siding. Checking your insurance policy is essential, as newer policies often **exclude asbestos** coverage due to its high cost. Asbestos abatement, especially in materials like spackle or plaster, can be extremely expensive, more often running into tens of thousands of dollars and even hundreds of thousands. Ensuring proper abatement is important to avoid health concerns.

It's advisable to review your policy and check for asbestos coverage (**more importantly, see if it is excluded**.) You might have the option to add an endorsement for coverage. **Keep in mind that asbestos coverage is part of your Coverage A,** and a major abatement can significantly reduce available funds for repairs and restoration in your home.

Ordinance & Law or Code Upgrade

When facing a loss in your home that necessitates a permit or the demolition of a room, and the wiring, although not damaged by the loss, is deemed old and must be replaced due to code requirements, it can incur additional expenses. If your insurance policy includes ordinance or law coverage, which is often a percentage of your policy, or if you've purchased it separately, you're covered for such code-related expenses. However, if your policy lacks ordinance or law coverage, you may have to personally cover the extra cost mandated by the code.

On substantial losses, particularly in older homes, requiring extensive electrical upgrades to meet current codes. If you need code requirements, like a sprinkler system if you have a 3rd floor, or you have ½ inch subfloors that now need to be 5/8 or ¾ inch, or an illegal basement that does not have an egress window, these expenses can be significant. It's important to consider these potential costs, and if your policy doesn't automatically include ordinance or law coverage, obtaining an endorsement is advisable. Investing in this endorsement can help you avoid unexpected out-of-pocket expenses associated with code compliance.

The majority of these code requirements fall with electrical and egress.

When it comes to electrical upgrades necessitated by code requirements, coverage is typically specific to the affected area. If one room in your house requires a wiring upgrade and you have ordinance & law coverage, it covers the incurred expenses for that particular area. However, it doesn't imply that the entire house's electrical system will be paid for by insurance.

The application of ordinance & law is incurred on a room-by-room or area basis. If the wiring issue is contained within a specific room, the code or ordinance work will remain confined to that space.

However, if the wiring needs to be extended to another area where it is connected, such as being daisy- chained or pigtailed, the costs for the additional work will be covered after the initial work is completed. It's important to clarify that insurance coverage for ordinance & law is handled on an incurred basis, with the initial code work covered and any supplementary costs for repairs (such as drywall or plaster). This ensures that the coverage is specific to the necessary upgrades and repairs directly related to the code requirements.

Regarding egress windows, particularly in northern regions, if you have a finished basement that lacks approval from the building department, it may impact your eligibility for code coverage. If the basement is considered illegal and not approved, you might not receive coverage for ordinance & law because it shouldn't have been finished in the first place. In such cases, the financial responsibility for the necessary modifications would likely fall on you.

If the building department possesses plans indicating that the basement was finished without an egress window, you may have the opportunity to be covered under ordinance and law by your insurance carrier. However, the carrier is likely to request documentation from the building department to verify the lack of an egress window, and their agreement or consideration may be contingent upon the availability of such documents. If the building department insists on compliance before certifying occupancy, you'll need to decide whether to remove the finished basement or undertake the required modifications to meet the building standards.

Cause & Origin

Determining the cause and origin of a fire involves an investigation to establish how it started. In the event of a fire at someone's residence, the fire marshal/fire department conducts their own inquiry to identify the root cause. Once the fire marshal reaches a conclusion and assesses the situation, they often clear the scene promptly unless there are suspicions of foul play.

However, the clearance by the fire marshal does not conclude the matter for the insurance company. They initiate their own investigation to ascertain whether the fire resulted from factors other than accidental causes. This step is important for potential subrogation, where the insurance company may pursue legal action against the responsible party or manufacturer. Essentially, while the insurance company settles the claim, they may seek reimbursement from the company or entity accountable for the incident. The timeline for entering the investigation scene can be brief, or the inquiry may extend for several weeks, depending on the complexity of the case.

(Subrogation extends to other incidents like water damage. For instance, if a recently purchased dishwasher malfunctions and causes water damage, the manufacturer of the dishwasher may be held responsible.)

Subrogation

Subrogation becomes relevant when the cause of loss is not the insured's fault but is attributed to an external entity, such as a contractor or the manufacturer of an appliance. There are various reasons for subrogation, and the process typically unfolds after your insurance company has settled your claim. The initiation of subrogation depends on the specifics of the loss and its cause.

However, it's important to clarify that subrogation may not apply uniformly in all cases. For instance, in a condominium complex, if a hot-water heater on the 12th-floor malfunctions, causing flooding on lower floors, the dynamics of subrogation can be influenced by the type of insurance—whether it's condominium or townhouse insurance. This is distinct from traditional homeowners insurance.

In certain situations, like the one described, subrogation might not come into play. Condominium and townhouse insurance considerations are different, recognizing the unique risks associated with different floors. If subrogation is applied uniformly in scenarios like this, insuring condos, particularly those on higher floors, could become impractical for insurance companies. In layman's terms, the 12th floor caused the loss. The carrier will not be paying for the losses below them. HOWEVER, If it was a hot-water heater that was newly installed and it was a manufacturing defect or installation error, then yes, there is the possibility of subrogation.

Water Damage & Should I File a Claim?

Addressing sudden water leaks in your home demands a swift and systematic response. Initially, your priority should be to halt the water flow, achieved either by shutting off the main water supply to your house or by isolating the affected area. Subsequently, reaching out to a plumber becomes a priority to identify the source and cause of the water.

Once the plumber assesses the situation, you face a decision. If the water damage is minor and contained, skipping an insurance claim might be prudent. Assess the damage in the area – is it manageable for you, or do you require professional assistance? In the latter case, consider contacting a mitigation company instead of immediately involving your insurance company. Your plumber may recommend a mitigation company. You can delay involving your insurance company as premature claims might lead to **unintended consequences**.

It is advisable to seek recommendations from your insurance company without initiating a claim if you're uncertain. This can help ensure that your rates don't go up in the future by making an unnecessary claim. Clear communication is essential – if there's no intent to file a claim right now, make that unequivocally clear during the call.

After the plumber diagnoses the issue and the mitigation company inspects the damage, a decision to file a claim must be well-considered. Remember, **filing a claim attaches to your history**, potentially affecting future rates and policy renewal. It's advisable to **reserve filing a claim for damages that will NOT exceed $10,000, factoring in your deductible. To better explain, your mitigation is going to cost you around $1500, and the repairs will be around $3000 for a total of $4500. You now have to factor in your deductible. If it is $500, then you will receive a $4000 Replacement Cost Value (RCV). Is $4000 enough for you to have a claim history for years to come and the possibility of higher rates plus paying out-of-pocket $500 to pay for the repairs? The increase in your rate can be much higher than the initial $4000 over the next few years. What if you have a $2500 deductible? Then you would only receive $2000 RCV and have to come out of pocket $2500. You need to take this into consideration as everyone's financial situation is different.**

In the event of a claim, meticulous documentation is paramount. Photograph the damaged areas, the source of the leak, and the repairs carried out by the plumber. This documentation will be critical in ensuring your claim's legitimacy and preventing any reasons for denial. **YOU MUST KEEP THE DAMAGED SOURCE, DO NOT DISCARD.**

Mitigation companies play a vital role in the process, conducting moisture readings, documenting damages, and initiating the drying process. They may offer repair services or, alternatively, you can choose your own contractor, though choosing a non-remediation contractor is discouraged due to their limited expertise in this area. Even if they tell you they have done them before, that does not mean they have enough experience to estimate your repairs and negotiate with an experienced adjuster. Nor do they know what to do in order to handle a claim that has a difficult adjuster and the avenues to navigate your claim if there are other problems. This will cause you to get less for your repairs than what you are owed.

Assuming the mitigation/remediation company handles repairs, estimates will be negotiated & agreed on, a project manager will be assigned to you, material choices need to be made, repairs will commence, and finally, a certificate of satisfaction is signed. Payment, often involving a deductible, concludes the process. The mitigation company then submits the necessary documents to your insurance company for approval, ultimately concluding your project.

FIRE DAMAGE

Let's discuss fire incidents. There are various approaches to handling fires, but we'll focus on two basic scenarios: a small kitchen or garage fire or a minor electrical outlet fire in a bathroom that initially affects only one room but spreads smoke throughout the entire home. In such situations, if the fire department is called, you may face a barrage of public adjusters and remediation contractors reaching out to you. They often try to contact you during the initial stressful moments, taking advantage of your distress and unfamiliarity with insurance processes.

It's important to resist the pressure to hire a public adjuster immediately, despite their insistence on the need for their services. Many times, they capitalize on your vulnerability. Instead, after dealing with the immediate aftermath of the fire, such as putting it out or waiting for the fire trucks to leave, the recommended course of action is to contact your insurance company and file a claim.

Consider reaching out to a mitigation company, either through personal recommendations or referrals. It's advisable to engage a mitigation company for house cleaning without relying on a public adjuster to dictate your choice. Numerous mitigation companies work with insurance providers, so contact at least three of them to discuss their services and determine the best fit for your needs.

Regardless of the mitigation company you choose, there will be a cause and origin investigation, so avoid touching or entering the area where the fire originated. The mitigation company will deploy air scrubbers and a crew to clean walls, ceilings, floors, contents, and soft goods throughout your home. Items like ornamental rugs may need specialized cleaning, covered by your contents coverage, and your insurance agent can provide relevant information.

Once the mitigation process is complete, the focus shifts to repairs. Estimates should include potential areas that need removal for thorough cleaning and odor elimination. For smaller fires, painting most walls and ceilings in your home is typically necessary. Note that casings, base moldings, doors, and crown molding may not need painting if they are coated with semi-gloss paint, which can be cleaned effectively.

Please take special note of high hats, as they are hollow, and smoke may have entered the ceiling behind drywall. Keep in mind that each fire incident is unique, and the way smoke/soot travels can vary. Tailor your approach to address the specific challenges presented by the fire incident you're dealing with.

Major Fire Damage

Now, let's discuss a significant fire – one that devastates you and your entire family. It is an extremely emotional and stressful experience. You witness everything you own being destroyed right in front of you. I'm going to take you through a detailed explanation of how this all works. And just remember, don't hire a public adjuster because, as you watch everything you have lost, these individuals are preying on your duress. Over the next few weeks, they aim to get you to sign with them. I'm telling you right now, they don't care about you; what they care about is your signature. I am a public adjuster, and for every loss I have dealt with, I convey the same advice.

I'm going to touch on a few topics here that have already been mentioned, so I won't go into great detail, but I'll explain the proper way and what you should do immediately if this unfortunate event happens to you.

Once everyone is out and safe and the fire trucks have arrived to contain the fire, your local gas company will turn off the gas, and the electrical company will be there to either clip the lines/lugs at the pole or pull your meter. If they do not clip the lines, they will pull your meter, and electricity cannot be restored without a licensed electrician. You should call your insurance company immediately, providing them with as much information as possible. But do not go back into the house. At the same time, there will be companies called board-up companies. That is the only company you need right away at this very moment to secure your property and protect it from people entering and from secondary damages such as snow, rain, and the environment. A public adjuster may claim they can get them there; don't fall for it.

Let your insurance company get a boarding company out there. Most likely, a boarding company is already waiting for you, as these services are needed immediately. You don't need to hire a public adjuster to have a boarding company secure your home. Call a board-up company or use the one on-site, but they are only there to board up, and you don't need to hear any recommendations or referrals from them either.

The next thing that should happen, possibly simultaneously, depending on the time of the fire and when people arrive, is calling an electrician experienced in providing emergency services to restore temporary power to the home and place string lighting throughout. If you are more interested in getting things back to order immediately, then you should be thinking about your architect. Because, no matter what, you will need an architect to draw up plans for the damages, and you have to file a permit with the building department. This can take two or three months to happen. You do not want to wait until a settlement has been negotiated and then have an architect come in. If you sign with a mitigation or restoration company, they will recommend an architect. But you should do this at the very beginning because, no matter what, this needs to be paid for and done. You should use an architect with experience in dealing with fires.

During this time, all of your belongings need to be inventoried – what is salvageable, non-salvageable, but what can be cleaned and stored. Have that set up? While this is all going on, and the inventory is scheduled, cause & origin has already been to your house. By now, your house has been inspected by an adjuster, and they're waiting for an answer on the cause & origin to clear the scene. If everything in your home is saturated, yes, you will want to move quickly on some sort of mitigation to reduce any additional secondary damages. However, if everything is destroyed, do not listen to a mitigation company telling you that it needs to be done right now because, ultimately, everything will be torn out and thrown out.

If you are in a warmer environment, you may want to have the wet items removed from the home as soon as possible to prevent mold from growing everywhere, as it becomes a health hazard if left for too long (within a week). This is a contradiction to what I just wrote, but for many different circumstances, minor mitigation may be required. Your insurance adjuster will come out to meet with you, sign the paperwork and go over everything. They will have their builder come out to write a repair estimate. Your contractor (who should be a remediation contractor) will also write their estimate. This process can take a couple of weeks. During that time, you should be in the mitigation process after the inventory, which means it's staged. Set up tables outside, inventory everything, throw it into a dumpster, sign a waiver to allow them to remove the dumpster of contents because it's all documented and photographed. They will now begin removing everything that was damaged. If it's a total gut, which most major fires are due to smoke, they will demo the entire interior of the home down to the studs. Then, they will wipe and clean everything and make it ready for repairs. What you do not want to do is have them spray and seal the home until any framing is completed. The reason is when framing gets done, it vibrates, and knocking will drop soot everywhere, and you will have the smell of smoke again. So, let the framing repairs be completed, and then you can spray, seal, and encapsulate the entire home as needed or required to prevent the smell of smoke in the future. If there is still an odor of smoke, then Ozone the house and that should prevent any further smell.

At this time, your estimates should have gone back and forth with the adjuster and the builder. They probably have come up with a common scope of repairs and an undisputed amount. If you have a mortgage on your home, the check will be written out to you and your mortgage company. You sign it and send it off to your mortgage company. Either one of two things will happen: they will send back a check, or they will disperse it in percentages to your contractor as they progress. Any changes, designing, or material selections are all done before you start your work. Once the repairs are completed, you sign a certificate of satisfaction. It's sent off to the insurance company, and the depreciation gets released to either you or the contractor, depending on who's invoicing.

Mitigation Companies

Mitigation companies play a crucial role in addressing property damage, especially when dealing with vendors of the carrier. However, when engaging with a non-vendor, it's essential to exercise caution.

Despite this, it's important to recognize that you, as the client, hold significant power in such agreements. When entering into contracts with non-vendors, be vigilant about potential charges exceeding what the insurance company allows. Prior to finalizing an agreement, consider raising a crucial question to the mitigation contractor: if the insurance company underpays, will you be held responsible for covering the difference? Request this clarification in writing or via email to establish a clear understanding beforehand.

In some instances, non-vendors have resorted to placing liens on a homeowner's property to recover unpaid balances or have threatened to do so. While the threat of a lien can be a negotiation tactic, it's crucial to distinguish between an idle threat and a genuine intention to proceed with such actions. It's reasonable for a mitigation contractor to seek payment, but their approach should align with ethical business practices.

In the age of social media, a homeowner's complaint and review carry significant weight. If faced with a mitigation company threatening to place a lien on your property, make it known that you are prepared to share your experience extensively. Mitigation companies, wary of negative reviews, are unlikely to follow through with a lien if they value their reputation. Ultimately, a company resorting to such extreme measures may not be suitable for the emergency fire and water restoration business.

FLOOD

Oct-2022 RR 2.0: Equity in Action NFIP Flood Insurance Manual (fema.gov)

F-122_October 2021 NFIP Dwelling Form SFIP (fema.gov)

https://www.fema.gov/fact-sheet/what-expect-when-you-apply-fema-assistance

The above links are to better help you with your questions about what flood actually covers.

Floods, being natural disasters, are excluded from standard insurance policies. To secure coverage for potential flood damage, individuals must separately purchase flood insurance, typically from their insurance carrier if it is offered. In cases where a carrier doesn't provide flood insurance, options include applying to FEMA for assistance or seeking coverage from a private flood insurance company 30 days prior to a flood, albeit at a potentially high premium.

It's important to note that all flood insurance is rooted in the National Flood Insurance Program (NFIP) administered by FEMA. NFIP coverage is designed to address essential needs for habitability and safety, focusing on items crucial for daily living ONLY. This encompasses key household components like boilers, water heaters, air conditioners, electrical and plumbing systems, and pumps. Additionally, coverage extends to appliances such as refrigerators, built-in ranges, washing machines, and dryers.

In instances where a basement is finished and sustains flood damage, NFIP coverage is limited to unfinished drywall. It's noteworthy that if individuals have flood insurance through their carrier, the coverage is structured similarly to NFIP. This holds true whether one resides in a flood zone or not.

Private flood insurance, while an option, often comes with a higher premium, but that coverage can be whatever that carrier wants to provide.

In summary, navigating flood insurance involves understanding the distinctions between NFIP and private coverage, recognizing the essentials covered for habitability, and being aware of potential limitations based on dwelling location and policy type. In layperson's terms, if you have a finished area below grade, you will only be covered for the essential systems in the home and unfinished drywall. If above grade, you will be covered for the only damaged items, so if half the kitchen cabinets got damaged, then only half of the cabinets will be replaced and no more. Private Flood Insurance is costly, yet not if you actually have a flood. You really need to read the terms and coverage when purchasing a private flood policy. If you have no flood insurance coverage, then your only option is to apply to FEMA for help.

Summary

For the simplest way to figure all of this out, and you don't want to go back and forth. There is a universal way to make sure you have enough money to do the work but it does require you to know two very important things.

1) How much will all of the material cost? and you Cannot miss ANYTHING.

2) How many labor days will it take to perform the Work? Averaging the labor days by $500 per day Per laborer.

Add 1 & 2 together and multiply by 1.71. This will give you a very good idea of the cost of any project.

It is not recommended but it is a good formula to figure out if you are being paid properly. You can use it to see if any future project is not related to a claim but to new work, renovation, remodel, or alteration. For high-end work with a large company, you should use $700 per day for labor.

We hope you got the information you needed to make an informed decision from this book. If you are looking for further assistance, please go to **claimhelpme.com**

On this site you will also be able to access 8 accurately written estimates for you to compare or use for vital information. Estimators can really benefit from these estimates & boost their careers.

Made in the USA
Middletown, DE
23 May 2024

54547970R00068